PURSUED

THE SWAMP #2

REBECCA ROYCE

Pursued (The Swamp #2)

Copyright @ 2019 by Rebecca Royce

Ebook ISBN: 978-1-951349-16-5

Print ISBN: 978-1-951349-21-9

Cover art by Syneca Featherstone at Original Syn

Content Editing: Heather Long

Copy/Proof Editing: Jennifer Jones

Final Proof Editing: Meghan Leigh Daigle

Formatting: Ripley Proserpina

Published by Rebecca Royce

www.rebeccaroyce.com

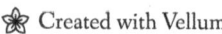 Created with Vellum

FOREWORD

Dearest Reader,

Hello! How are you? I hope this note finds you well. You are currently reading the forward to Book two in the Swamp series. This is the second book of three, and this book is absolutely not meant to be read alone. I cannot stress that enough. If you haven't read book one, please don't read book two, and then get really angry that the story didn't make sense. It really won't if you haven't read book one.

Also, this book ends without a happy ending, but let me be clear—book three, Caught, will end happily. I'm stressing that again. This. Book. Does. Not. Have. A. Happy. Ending. It may even end on a cliffhanger. Book three will tie up loose ends and make a happy ending. Please don't send me hate filled PMs at seven in the morning before I've had coffee telling me how angry you are about this.

I am going to point right to this forward and show you where I warned you.

I love MacKenzie, Rainer, Preston, Jarret, and Anton. I hope you do, too. I hope you'll stay with me through book three, and I hope that in the end, you'll love them as I do. I love you all for reading, taking chances with my books, and being the best readers imaginable. You humble me every day.

Warmest regards and with gratitude that you are reading this,

Rebecca Royce

ONE

I stepped out of the trailer into the woods, aware something was about to go terribly wrong. I'd gotten good at telling when that was going to happen. Maybe it was part of my ever-developing Omega powers. Maybe it was just that everything went wrong so frequently for me that the feeling meant I was right about that more times than I wasn't.

"Kenzie?" my brother said from the couch. "Close the door. You're letting the mosquitos in."

I shut it abruptly. I did hate the summer bugs. Sitting on the steps of the trailer, I thought about all the things we'd done to arrive at this moment. Of course, I had no idea if this was really the moment we'd been waiting for to happen for the last three weeks, or if it was just another false alarm.

We'd been running nonstop, and today was the first time we'd both felt ready to fend off an attack should one come for us. I closed my eyes and breathed, letting my wolf senses wander. I was a werewolf. Kind of an important one when it came down to it—the first Omega born in a generation. In fact, the lack of Omegas had caused the packs to insist that werewolves live like humans and stop shifting, lest they risk insanity and become the much-feared Loup-Garou. It turned out that without an Omega, a pack was basically sick, and sick packs made Loups.

I'd spent a huge amount of time fixing that. Everywhere I went, Loups appeared, and I healed them. That was my job. It was like they could scent me from great distances and went out of their way to find me. Night after night, state after state. They came, seeming scary but really just needing my help.

None of this had happened before I was kidnapped from my home, forced to shift, rescued, and brought to Louisiana to be hidden away by the Lejeune brothers. It was there everyone discovered I was the Omega, it was there I'd stumbled upon the extraordinary fact that the Lejeunes—Rainer, Preston, Jarret, and Anton—were my mates. There, the men who had secretly been controlling the fate of all wolves for far too long had forcibly ripped my mates from me.

My mates hunted me now, but to kill me rather than love me—thanks to whatever madness had gripped them due to Brennan, and the hell he'd descended down on us in order to satisfy some sort of corporations that wanted us dead. None of it made sense to me.

I opened my eyes. Yes, my senses were on full alert. I knocked four times in rapid succession to let Agustin know of my fears. That was our signal. Four fast taps. His chair scraped backward as he prepared for what might be coming.

We'd bought a used trailer from a less than reputable seller, and then proceeded to cut up the credit card we'd borrowed from one of my fathers-in-law so that it couldn't be traced. Since then, we'd driven place to place while we put together the only plan I could come up with that had a chance of winning. If there ever had been a rumor of werewolves living in a certain area, we went there and checked. In the meantime, we also built a cage. My brother had always been handy. It was amazing what he could do with materials we picked up in junkyards and tools he had *borrowed* from places. I didn't ask too many questions.

We Harpers had never been the type to steal from anyone. It was amazing how desperation drove us. I'd taken mental notes of the things we'd acquired. I was going to see to it that everyone got paid back. Somehow.

Losing my mates had nearly killed me. The marks they'd given me had abruptly disappeared, signaling physically what I'd known emotionally to be the case. After that, the emptiness pulled me under, and for two days, my brother hadn't been sure whether I'd wake up, or if I'd die where I shook on the bed.

When I'd come to, it had been with this idea. My last-ditch effort to try and see if there was any way in hell I could recapture what I'd had. So far, we hadn't stumbled on any werewolves except the Loups, and they were so confused, most of them having been ousted from packs decades earlier, they were never much help knowing where werewolves should be.

The question had to be asked. Were the wolves all hiding so we couldn't find them, or had the same group that now had my husbands taken them? I rubbed my eyes. I had no way of knowing.

A plodding sound caught my attention, and I leaned against the door. That wasn't my mates. I sniffed the air, knowing what I'd find before I laid eyes on the man. It was a Loup.

I knocked three times. Truth was, I didn't need my brother to help me with this. I'd gotten really good at it.

Rising from where I sat, I stared at the sick wolf. My

hands burned. That used to be painful. Now, I knew the difference. The burn was nothing. It was the pain that would come later that was going to be the problem.

"Hi." I'd taken to speaking to the men who came. I wasn't sure they could understand while they were like this. It simply made me feel better. "So, you are my first Loup in Indiana. That means you get to be Loup number one in the journal we're keeping. I don't know why it matters that I keep track of this. Maybe someday it will."

He clomped on two feet. That was the problem with Loups. They no longer moved or looked like werewolves, but they weren't human either, not when they were like this. They couldn't control their shifts and had no memory of what happened to them.

The Loup swiped at me when I was close. He needed me, but he didn't know why he'd come, much less have any awareness of what I could do for him.

My brother stepped out of the trailer. "Feisty one, huh?"

"Don't judge. Hopefully, you'll never be in his situation, and I might point out that when you needed my help, you nearly killed me. It's par for the course."

His answer was silence, and I winced. "Sorry, Agustin. I know I'm sniping at you. I'm not..."

"I know, Kenzie." He took another step down. "I'm not upset with you, and you're right. I have no business making fun of anyone. I love you."

He really must, or he would have taken off and never come back weeks earlier. The empty place in my soul whipped around, threatening to take down anyone in its path. That was always Agustin. And, silently, always me.

I'd gone dark in a way that I'd never imagined I was capable of.

But none of that would help me now. I approached the Loup again. "I can shift and we can do this that way, but for my own selfish sake, I'd rather not. I'm going through way too many clothes."

Maybe he liked the sound of my voice, because I doubted he could actually understand what I said. I placed my hand on his arm. My power rushed into the Loup. We stood there, and I closed my eyes. This was going to take as long as it took.

In my mind's eye, I could see the power fixing what was wrong with him, bringing his wolf—the real one, not the twisted kind that had taken its place—to the surface again. Werewolves needed to shift regularly. End of story. Some people could endure the assault of not shifting better than others. This wasn't their fault. There had always been Loups, mostly packless lone wolves who had fallen on hard times. But the huge numbers of them could be directly blamed on a werewolf named Brennan, and the bargain he'd struck with the rich children of werewolf hunters who wanted to use us for their own nefarious means.

Right in the middle was me. The Omega they wanted to own, or wanted to kill, or maybe it was both. I'd given up obsessing over what that was. By taking my mates from me, they'd essentially killed something inside of me. With this constant running, they effectively owned me, too. Maybe this was all the point. They'd never send anyone after me, I'd never get the chance to save my loves, and I'd forever be running from no one.

I pushed away the dark thoughts. The Loup needed light from me. Not angst. If such a thing was possible.

We stood there for a long time, so much so that the cicadas in the area grew even louder, singing through the night. My brother had told me they only appeared in this area every seventeen years. I didn't know if we were lucky we got to hear them or unlucky, since they made it really hard for me to sleep, something I desperately needed. Tomorrow we would leave. Pushing to Ohio to see if we could find any werewolves there.

Finally, the Loup gasped. It was the signal he'd healed. He fell backward, shifting into his human form as he hit the ground. The suddenness of not having to feed him power caused me to shake. My brother grabbed onto me before I could fall.

"I'll get him out of here. See if he knows anything."

I doubted he would. "Thanks."

Healing the Loup left me weak, shaken. Without my mates' support, I'd be even emptier inside. I had no guide-book to teach me how to be an Omega, but I'd bet that Omegas were not supposed to be alone. We were meant to have mates to love. Mine had filled me up inside, so the constant cold of what was wrong in the world couldn't over-take me.

A smell hit my nose just as I turned to head up the stairs in our trailer. It was metallic, sick, the scent that permeated my nightmares and had me waking up choking every single night. I knew that scent. I whipped around.

Leaning against a tree was my second oldest mate, Preston. He'd lost some of the frosted tips he had in his hair. I blinked. How ridiculous was it that I noticed that of all things? The second thing that struck me as I was digesting the first was that his eyes were cold, blank. Preston was here, but it wasn't really Preston here. He didn't even have a scent, nothing other than the metal.

My brother jumped to his feet, dragging the former Loup with him.

I swallowed through the lump in my throat as my hands started burning again.

"You did just what the fuck I thought you would. I dragged the stupid Loup fifty miles to get him here. But it was worth the effort just to watch you use up all your ridiculous power on him, and know that you'd have none left for me."

He hadn't moved. Preston leaned against the tree like it was a lazy Sunday, and he had nowhere to go.

"I see you found us." This was what I had wanted. One of my mates had arrived alone. More than just one, and I wouldn't have had a chance of doing what I likely couldn't do anyway. Seeing him was an assault. It was as though I had a festering wound that was never going to close, never going to go away, and his arrival was akin to him taking his finger and shoving it in the wound itself.

We'd only been apart three weeks, and yet that particular wound would never heal.

It might have helped if Preston hadn't looked so delicious. He was a beautiful man. Tall, dark haired with those blond tips he'd loved so much, or without them, and strong.

"Get that poor man out of here, Agustin." My brother nodded, and I appreciated him not arguing with me. Whatever was about to happen couldn't take place with a stranger here, not one still weak from a decade in hell.

Without another word, Agustin dragged the unconscious man away. Preston followed him with his gaze.

"We don't care whether we get your brother back or not, so if he interferes with this, he's dead. End of story. I told them if I could arrange to exhaust you, you wouldn't fight at all." He walked toward me. The empty inside of me roared to life, threatening to lash at this imposter wearing Preston's body. I forced my mouth to stay shut.

"I told them," he continued. "That you were a weak fucking girl. Relatively powerless, despite your Omega abilities. Not strong as a wolf. I explained how you were mediocre at best and could barely handle yourself when it came to being Omega. How I'd always wondered if you were some kind of genetic mistake, because surely no one as pathetic as you could be an Omega." He smelled the air. "Yes. I was right. One Loup, and you're done. What's the matter, Mac? If we're not with you to hold your hand, you can't handle the smallest things?"

These weren't Preston's words any more than it had been my brother trying to kill me when he'd been under their control. Still, I'd have been lying if I said it didn't wound to hear them. Once again, he poked my festering wound.

I let myself look at him. He wore a black high-necked t-shirt and a blue pair of jeans. He'd put on a pair of boots I'd never seen him in before.

"My brother won't interfere. He's going to take the Loup far from here. You can leave him alone."

Preston rolled his eyes. "I'm just here for you, and I'm glad I came. Such a relief to have my life back, and not have to be your stupid mate. A person can convince themselves anything is okay. That is what I did with you. I settled. Being here with you, it reminds me full on how lucky I am to be rid of you. Come without a fuss, and it doesn't have to hurt when they have you. Give me a hard time, and I'll see that it does."

I wanted to shift, rub up against his leg, mark myself with his scent, fix what had been broken. The empty in me wanted to tear at him until he knew the kind of pain he inflicted on me. Instead, I walked calmly toward him. There was a plan for this. We hadn't expected the Loup to be here, but I trusted my brother to do his part. We counted on each other. Forgave each other. In only the way that family born not just of genetics, but of the heart could. Preston was supposed to be that, too.

"You want me to come with you. To walk out of these woods and just... go with you to whichever lab they've instructed you to take me. I'm just supposed to comply, because I'm weak and tired. Because I loved the person you used to be. Because I'm... *pathetic*."

Preston gave me a cold smile. "Even now, I can scent your desperation. Don't fight it, Mac. You're nothing without us, and it's time to put nothing to bed."

I nodded. "You're right. I am kind of a lousy wolf. Easily tired. Untrained as a werewolf. My Omega powers are flimsy at best. Everything you said to me was correct, and I'll tell you what, Preston. I'm not foolish, so I know I'd never take you in a fight. Not even if I was at full power. You're a strong, tough werewolf. Once, I would have counted on you to save me."

"I'm hearing a but, and that is stupid." He narrowed his eyes. "Don't make me follow secondary protocol and kill you. That would be such a waste of resources."

"The but you're hearing is simple. I don't have the slightest intention of fighting you like a werewolf."

He never heard the shot, but the second the tranquilizer hit him in the shoulder, he realized what had happened.

I tilted my head to stare at him. He'd be down in seconds. "My brother and I grew up in rural Colorado. You have to imagine the coyote problem we used to have. Even in the suburban parts of the area. We couldn't shift to deal with it, and Agustin never had the stomach to kill anything. We raised chickens, and damn it, one of my fathers didn't want them dead. They made eggs." I smiled. "Agustin got really adept at shooting them with tranqs from his bedroom window."

Preston fell backward, and I didn't try to stop him. He was right. I was feeling really weak. I leaned forward. "I'm afraid I lied when I told you that Agustin wouldn't interfere. You must not be much of a wolf like this, Preston. I can't believe you didn't smell it."

His eyes rolled to the back of his head. I looked over my shoulder toward the woods. We'd been hiding the tranq guns everywhere we went for the last three weeks. "The Loup was helpful; it gave us a way we wouldn't have otherwise had."

Trying to find a reason why Agustin would run off to the woods and leave me had been a problem we hadn't worked out. But now that this was done, I wasn't sure we needed to have worried. This wasn't thinking, reasoning Preston. This was a shell of the man I loved. A creature wore his body, followed instructions, and not much else. Sure, he'd reasoned that he could bring me the Loup, but that had probably come under the direction of "trick her into coming, or something like that."

"What did you do with the Loup?" I tried really hard never to learn their names. This was a job for me, not a calling. Granted, I'd have to do it for the rest of my life, but I wasn't interested in becoming too emotionally invested. Why should I, when I had my own emptiness to live with? It threatened to drag me under, to rip me apart, to swallow me whole.

Agustin sighed. "Why do you care what I did with him, if you are so completely disinterested in them?"

We'd been having this argument for weeks. "Fine. Don't tell me."

"He's safely in the woods. He'll wake up and find his

way home. They all do. I gave him fifty dollars to get him something to eat, and a bus ticket out of here. We're three miles from the main road. He'll be fine."

I nodded. "Would you mind dragging Preston up and putting him in the cage?"

Agustin strode over to my former mate and stared down at him. "You ready for this? You just took down a Loup."

"I'm going to shower and eat before I get going."

The truth was now that I'd gotten to this point, I wasn't sure I could do it at all. My hands burned, my body ached to fix what was wrong, and it wasn't going to be a physical problem for me to do this. The hesitation was something else entirely.

I rubbed my neck where his mark used to be. The first days without him—without all of them—had been akin to death. Whoever I was on the other end of it wasn't the same as the girl I'd been the day before. Mating was supposed to be eternal. I guessed it was for everyone but me. Nothing was certain, and my existence in this life felt like walking on gelatin instead of concrete.

"He might wake up."

I shrugged. "If he wakes up, he wakes up."

"Kenzie." He visibly swallowed. "This isn't Preston. The things he said are not him any more than when I tried to tear out your neck. It's compulsion based on mind control."

Agustin dragged Preston into the cage and set him down before he locked him in. I stared at him for a second. He'd changed his clothes. I don't know why I was so fixated on that. Somehow, in my head they were mindless, locked up, and still exactly as I'd last seen them. But here he was. Showered. Clean. In clothes I didn't know he owned.

But then, I'd never once looked in Pres' closet.

"We don't really know each other. We all just kind of gave in to the mating, as though it was a given. I don't, for example, know his birthday or his favorite color. We've never eaten at a restaurant together. Been on a date. Watched a movie."

Agustin put his hand on my arm. "That is how mating works. The rest of it comes after you acknowledge the mating. Yours just got a little heightened because of the danger. With years ahead of you, Sister, you will know those things. Those men? I could smell their love for you."

My brother was many things, but psychic was not one of them. I didn't have the slightest idea how to explain to him what I couldn't really understand myself. Every day... the emptiness ate more of me.

"I won't be terribly long about it."

He nodded. "Whatever you need, little sister."

I'd really lucked out in the brother department. All four of them were gems. I just had to somehow figure out how to not destroy all of my relationships. If I couldn't feel love, then I'd fake it.

Somehow.

Despite what I told him, I lingered in the shower, letting the hot water roll over me. I washed my hair. Twice. Shaved everywhere I could think of, and took my time with the blow-dryer. I stared in the mirror. I'd worried that I had become unrecognizable and expressed that to Rainer. This was so much worse.

It was like my eyes belonged to someone else.

Agustin knocked on the door. "I checked him for trackers. None on him."

My brother hadn't had any either. But sooner or later they would start sending someone to us with a tracker. We'd have to figure out what to do about that.

"Thanks," I called back.

"Going to get going now. Give me a minute to detach the hot water line and what not. I'll be fast."

For this to work, to stay one step ahead of all of this, we had to keep moving. He would get us on the road to Ohio while I took care of Preston. Where we went from there was questionable. Just as long as we kept moving.

I dressed in comfortable clothes, not that I had any others. Yoga pants. Sweats. One pair of jeans, but I didn't dare wear them, lest I had to shift and rip them apart. I liked them too much. I had three pairs of sneakers and a variety of ugly t-shirts. I'd given up wearing underwear. I had one bra, in case I actually had to see people, then I'd put it on so that I had some support.

I padded out into the main room, gripping onto the side of the table when we took a sharp turn. My brother didn't handle this thing as well as I did. But since I was the only one who could do the next step, it was up to me to do it.

My whole body ached like one giant wound. The shower hadn't helped. Nothing ever did. I made it over to the fridge. It was small, but it worked. We'd cooked up some noodles the day before. I would reheat them.

"Isn't this cozy?" Preston's voice filled the room.

I looked over my shoulder. "Hungry?"

TWO

He sat in the cage like being locked in one was no big deal, as though it were just a matter of normalcy for him. He tilted his head to look at me with his dead eyes, and it was everything I could do to not shift and rip them out of his head. Who was this imposter wearing his body? Just a nasty, mean version of Preston? Were his words a reflection of Preston's real thoughts? A kind of raw honesty *my* Preston would never have said aloud?

I put the pasta in the small microwave and waited for it to ding. My brother had charged us up at the last stop, and these new trailers had an amazing power cell that lasted a long time. Still, I was using a lot of power and needed to back off a bit. I sighed. Wondering whether Preston really thought the things he now spit out of his mouth were the truth was going to get me nowhere. We all had dark sides. Mine floated precariously close to the surface these days, and keeping it down had become practically a full-time job. The Omega couldn't be wicked, couldn't be unkind, couldn't be the worst versions of ourselves. I didn't think. I had no one to tell me anything, and I made this up as I went along.

The pasta did not taste as good on reheat, and I quickly threw it in the garbage. The last thing I needed was for something to turn my stomach worse than it already was.

"Why are you bothering with this? We both know that you're worthless. You're some kind of mistake. The Omegas are gone. You shouldn't be here, and your complete lack of ability to do your role is evidence of this." He touched his chest. "I was their last effort to be nice to you. After me? They're going to come with guns. They're going to shoot you down and call it a day. Agustin, too. They obviously know about this RV, know about you running for your lives, that's how I caught you. No, Mac, I don't want food. Cut the pretense. You can't save anyone, and keeping me in this cage is pointless."

My stomach clenched. Funny thing was, he wasn't saying anything to me that I didn't already say to myself. I was terrible at this, and I didn't have anyone to negatively compare myself to. I just knew it.

"All right, you're not hungry. So I suppose that we should just get down to it."

He shook his head. "You know the second you approach this cage I'm just going to overtake you. You don't have me, or my brothers, to do the hard work for you. Face it, Mac, you're just worthless without us. Your brother is driving this piece of shit you're tooling around the country in."

I walked to the cage. I had to be in my human form to open it, and I knew he wasn't lying. He'd be on me in a hot second, ready to bring me down before he took out my brother in order to complete his task. There was just one thing he didn't know. I hadn't slept in three weeks. Well, not more than thirty-minute stretches. The pain in my body was constant. Whatever was going on with me, psychically or physically, I'd managed to continue to use my Omega powers whenever called upon.

I wasn't great at it, but I was competent, and that would be true whether or not I had Preston attacking me at the same time. He could harm me, and I'd fix him anyway while he did it.

"When this is over, just know that I don't blame you."

I don't know what terrible thing he would have said, because I flipped open the latch with that remark and shifted as fast as I could into my wolf form.

Preston was faster. He always had been. Years of experience, and maybe natural ability, simply made him better at it. It didn't matter. I hadn't expected to beat him, and it would have been easier for me to do this as a human, but if he got his claws or teeth in me like that, I was in deep trouble.

I didn't want to bleed to death.

I was empty and angry... not suicidal.

We tore at each other with our fangs. Him trying to stop me from saving him, and me attempting to push my power into him, healing him until the will to hurt me subsided. I don't know how long we wrestled like that. Pain was my constant friend, and Preston knew how to inflict it. I was losing blood. My body would heal in my werewolf form, but it wasn't going to be pretty. He tore off a piece of my fur. I growled at him but didn't let go. I could see it in his dead eyes, this Preston didn't know if he wanted to kill me, or if he wanted to take me back to his masters. Right now, it could go either way.

I had no intention of letting that happen.

I might hate my lot in life, but I was the motherfucking Omega.

We snapped and fought each other until I couldn't be sure if it was the RV that was moving or us. Still, I held on and wouldn't let go. I sent my power into him. This was worse that Agustin had been. They'd really amped Preston up.

Eventually, he sagged. The fight was leaving him, and his own cells were returning to normal. I held onto him, keeping my fur against his own. He whimpered, and I might have felt sorry for him if I wasn't convinced I might fall apart when this was over. He hurt? Well, so did I.

Preston collapsed on the floor. His scent returned to normal, that woodsy, cloves driven scent that I loved so much. He was back, clean of the medication that I believed in my totally unscientific mind kept him under their control. Others had been chipped, but as far as I knew, not Preston. Something made him susceptible, and they played on that weakness.

He shifted back, but he never woke up. His eyes stayed closed. I somehow forced the shift on myself, feeling every break of my bones, every reshaping of my muscles. I panted, naked on the ground. It took me a while to have enough strength to even crawl over to him. My powers didn't react. He was okay, albeit he couldn't be comfortable in the awkward, twisted position I'd left him in. I took a second to grab a pillow from the couch we'd somehow not damaged and placed it under his head. I laid him flat, and he immediately started snoring.

The sound almost made me laugh. That was such a Preston thing. It must have meant he was deep in a healing sleep.

"You okay?" Agustin sounded frantic, his voice shaky as he called from the front seat where he drove our massive vehicle down life's highway.

Was I? "Still alive, and he's fixed."

"I almost drove off the road. I know we agreed I'd leave this to you, but still. I thought he might kill you."

I spit, and blood came out of my mouth. Well, that was a new disgusting thing. "He almost did. Preston is nothing if not strong."

I managed to pull myself to my feet and unsteadily grabbed a long t-shirt. It would do for now. A place inside of me, hidden deep beneath the empty, begged me to just curl up next to Preston and lie with him. But the empty was louder, and soon I couldn't hear the other suggestion at all. I limped into the front and climbed in the passenger seat. "He'll be a powerful ally to have as we take them out one by one."

Agustin lifted an eyebrow. "Your mate? I think he'll be more than that, love. He's yours."

"He was. But I have no mates anymore. Markless. The mating died. We are... something else. Former mates?"

My brother shook his head. I could smell that he thought my answer was incredulous, and it made my nose itch. I leaned back in the seat. Could I sleep? Maybe, but it wouldn't be for very long. Was it even worth trying? There had been a time when I'd felt different after using my powers. Tired but full. Protected.

"I don't know what happened to lose your mark. Mates keep them even after death. But you aren't mateless. You have four of them, and while we bring these fuckers to their knees, you'll get them back. Try calling Preston your former mate to him. See what happens."

My brother might have thought it ridiculous, but I planned to do just that. I doubted Preston would care. Even if he still had my bite on his neck. Why was that? Why had mine vanished, and his stayed?

"I'm going to close my eyes."

"Good." He smiled at me. "Things will get better now. I believe that. You'll see."

My brother was an optimist. I wasn't.

I DREAMED of a woman standing in the ocean. The tide was low, but it rushed up to her ankles. "Please," she called to me. "I'm drowning in pain. I won't make it another year like this."

I stared at her. I'd never seen this woman before in my life, but like every shifter that visited me in my dreams, she needed my help. "Just shift. Call your wolf back. Do it. Break the Accords. You'll feel better."

Tears rushed down her face. "I can't. My wolf is gone. I need you, Omega. I need you. Please."

I could feel her pain in every part of her body, the way she was dying, moment by moment, because everything she was had dried up and gone. "Where are you?"

"California." She reached for me. "Where are you?"

"Not there."

I JOLTED AWAKE, my heart in my stomach. My brother turned the RV into a rest stop. "I need to pee. Sorry if I woke you."

"You didn't." And even if he had, I'd be grateful. That one had hurt. Who was I kidding? They all hurt. "Where are we?"

"Nowhere near where we need to be." He shrugged. "You slept about twenty-five minutes. Kenzie, you can't continue like this. You need to sleep at night. I'm going to leave the RV parked here and get some sleep myself after I pee."

I rolled my eyes at him. "Because I'm deliberately trying not to. Thought it would be fun to be sleep deprived. Thanks for the fucking help. Yes, go pee."

He sighed loudly, and this time I ignored him. My empty had whipped him, and I wasn't even sorry. Did that mean I was losing ground? Giving into the evil?

Would I even know if that happened?

Or worse, if it did, would I even care?

I managed to stumble out of the RV without disturbing Preston, who still snored on the floor where I'd left him. I was halfway to the bathroom, when I realized I wasn't wearing pants. It was the stares that reminded me, and I quickly turned and ran back inside before someone called the cops on me for indecency. Dressed, I ran out to use the bathroom and returned in record time.

The RV had a small separate bedroom in the back. I hadn't spent much time in it, but rather than watch Preston sleep, I crawled into the full-sized bed to stare at the ceiling.

My brother wasn't kidding when he said he meant to spend the night at the rest stop. When he came back from the men's room, he didn't pull the RV back on the road. If I'd thought it was safe, I'd offer to drive.

Instead, I listened to the sounds of the highway and pretended that somehow, everything would be okay.

"I NEED TO SEE YOUR SISTER." Preston's voice filtered into the room. I wasn't sleeping. Hadn't even a little bit, but I didn't feel like moving. I'd saved him and wanted him back. Now? I wasn't sure how I was going to deal with him at all. What was there to say?

I was supposed to keep them safe, keep them healthy, and I unequivocally failed.

"I know, but hold off a second. I doubt she's sleeping. I'm sure she can hear us, and yet it's still really important we talk about her."

There was a pause. "We can talk about her later. I need to see her now. Get out of my way before I hurt you."

Agustin sighed loudly. "Don't say I didn't try to warn you. Keep in mind, she hasn't slept more than brief half hour spurts in a month. The need for her is increasing every day and... well, I'll let you figure out the rest."

Preston tore into the room. I wasn't even sure he'd listened to the last bit of my brother's warning.

I sat up in the bed. I'd never gotten under the covers. He stared at me for a moment and rushed forward, but I held out my hand, and he got the message that meant I wanted him to stop. "Don't touch me okay? Everyone touches me, and when I'm not needed, I don't want anyone touching me."

Preston's scent deepened, like he'd suddenly paid very close attention to what I'd said. "Ah... okay. Sure. Mac, are you... sweetheart, I am so sorry. I can't express to you how completely distraught I am about what happened. I know that I wasn't in control of myself, but that doesn't mean that I don't feel like I... like I let you down."

His apology wasn't needed. This wasn't his fault, or on him in any way. "Obviously, none of this is on you. I'm glad I was able to help you. We'll have to figure out what to do to get all the other wolves they have, too. I'm not sure what you remember from what happened, if anything. Agustin said it's a little bit like trying to wade through pea soup all around you."

Preston rapidly blinked. "That's actually a very good description. Hold on a second." He ran a hand through his hair. "Are you okay? You don't smell right. Are you hurt?" He reached for me again, and I backed away toward the headboard. "What's happened? Did I harm you? I can hardly remember it. Like waking up from a... yes, pea soup dream of some kind. I can't explain. My last concrete memory was in our home in Louisiana. Mac?"

I had thought about this conversation I would have with the Lejeunes a million times in the last month. At no time had I imagined it would take place in the cramped room.

"What's going on?" I didn't know what to do, so the empty did it for me. I pulled down my shirt so he could see my neck and upper chest area. "This is what is going on. Okay? Do you understand now?"

He widened his eyes. "What the fuck?"

Preston reached out like he was going to touch my chest where his mark should have been. I backed up, hitting the bed behind me but fortunately, not falling over. "No touching."

"Mac," his voice broke, and I turned my back to grab a pair of shorts from the small drawer. "Where are your mating marks?" He rushed past me and looked in the mirror. "Mine is still there."

"I know." Fully dressed, I got out of the bed and walked into the living room. "Hungry?"

My brother must have pulled us back onto the road. I hadn't even noticed. Preston followed me into the room. "I'm a little hungry. Are you? I'll make something."

"There's nothing to make, not really. We can microwave

some dinners, but we need to be careful about power. Do you want the chicken one or the turkey one?"

He breathed hard. "Mac, please look at me. What is going on? What happened? What did they do to us?"

I sighed. He was right. This was avoidance of the worst kind. "I don't know if it was one or two days after you were... changed... the worst pain I could have imagined struck me down. For days I lay near death's door, and my marks were taken from me."

"That doesn't make any sense. The marks don't go away, even with death. My mother still has Joe's." His face fell. "And presumably still has Kevin's." He looked away.

My heart clenched. "I am so sorry that he's gone. I would have gladly done something if I could have."

"I know you would have." He reached for my hand, but I didn't take his offering. "Who took the marks? How did they go?"

I laughed, throwing my head back. "Who controls any of this? The marks were taken from me by whoever decided I should have them in the first place. They ripped them from me the same way you were all ripped from me. So I'm sorry you still have the mark, because that makes it more complicated than if we were all done to begin with. I'm sure yours will just fade away. And we can end this sham. So please don't touch me, don't come near me, you should leave if that's too hard. But I have to rescue the entire wolf world, mateless, and we both know I'm not much of an Omega."

His mouth fell open, and I turned on the microwave to warm up the chicken. It was tasteless, but 1 had to put food in my stomach to face whatever hell the rest of this day required.

"MacKenzie Harper." The use of my full name was what made me turn around. He never did that.

I lifted my eyebrows. "Yes?"

"I don't know what the fuck happened that made the marks go away. But let me assure you that none of this was a sham. Not one minute of it. Ever. You are my mate. And I know my brothers feel the same way. You are ours. This was always real, and still is."

He didn't understand. "It's over, Preston. And maybe you should consider yourself lucky."

He held up his hand. "Don't say that. Don't ever say anything like that to me again. I am lucky I got you, and this isn't you. Your whole scent is off, like you're sick. I need you to let me take care of you until we can figure out what happened."

Pain shot through me, burning all the way to my fingertips. Nausea rolled up, and I almost puked. "Agustin, stop. We have to get off the road here." I could feel the need to go somewhere. Like I'd known Preston was coming. Sometimes, I knew things before I should. The how and why confused me. I didn't understand it.

Preston placed a hand on my shoulder. I didn't mind it. The sense was actually a relief. Something else to focus on. The microwave chose that moment to ding. Oh, that was right. In addition to explaining to Preston why our life was not going to be our life, and handling some kind of wolf-slash-psychic experience, I'd also put chicken in the microwave.

"What is happening to you? What does your wolf say?"

My chin wobbled as I tried to answer him. I hadn't realized tears were so close to the surface, or that I even had any left to shed. I waited a beat to steady myself. My brother must have listened. The RV was getting off the highway.

"Where am I going, Kenzie?" Agustin yelled to me.

I swallowed. "Keep going straight when you get off the highway. I'll tell you when to turn."

I was like a beacon heading to who knew where. Preston waited for me to answer him. He really was so gorgeous. I could look at him all day but that would only make my heart break harder. "I don't feel my wolf at all, except if I have to shift to manage an Omega need. But how I feel as that wolf is different, too. I'm broken, Preston. Maybe the universe just meant to spare you the fallout."

He hugged me. I'd distinctly asked him not to touch me, but since I'd given in on that, I didn't open my mouth to complain. How could I, when it turned out to be the best hug I'd ever had? "How is your wolf?"

Preston shuddered in my arms. "Begging to come out, begging to take care of you. But we're going to stay on two feet for now. Where are you taking us?"

"To more pain. Wherever we end up... that's all there is anymore, and all there is to look forward to."

He pulled back, taking my cheeks in his hands. "Let's eat that mediocre smelling chicken, and then let's talk about why you're not sleeping. Okay? Those things first. Pain. And exhaustion. And missing the people you love. And thinking that people you love are essentially dead... that could make anyone feel lost and depressed. So, small steps. I don't know what happened to our marks. They aren't my biggest concern right now."

"Preston, it would be the easiest thing in the world to turn over all my problems to you. I'd love to just hand them to you, and know that you'll take care of me. But I won't survive losing your mark again. It will kill me. Better to leave it be. And let me be the empty I've become."

He didn't remark on that statement, moving past me to take the chicken out of the microwave. We needed to go left, and I told Agustin that. Preston found the plates I'd forgotten we had and spooned the runny chicken onto a plate for me.

"You have to eat, too." I took the plate from him.

He side-eyed me staring at the contents in our small fridge before grabbing a bottle of water. "Pretty sure I've been well fed but, yes, I will eat. I'll do the turkey. Go sit down."

I did, because I wasn't sure that my knees weren't about to give out. "I know I seem wrong. Different." I sat down and spooned some of the sauce into my mouth with the utensils he handed me. "I know that. And I can't do anything about it. I'm empty."

"You've used that word before. And there was a solution to it. But we'll deal with that later." The microwave beeped again, and he took out his turkey. After a minute of fooling with it, he sat down across from me at the little table. "You've lost ten pounds. Maybe more. Whatever is happening, you have to eat. Promise me that much?"

I nodded. "Sometimes it's hard. The pain makes it hard."

"Your body just hurts?" He chewed very fast and swallowed.

I set down my fork. "It just hurts."

We were almost wherever I needed Agustin to go. I called out to him. "Can you pull over?"

"We're in some town. Sure. I'll find a space. Maybe we'll steal someone's wallet and eat in a restaurant."

My brother and I had become nefarious. I never could have imagined it. Preston choked. "I have a lot of money."

"No, you can't use it. They'll trace you with it. Whoever these men are, they're powerful."

Preston rubbed his eyes. "That's right. It's not clear.

Like that pea soup thing but, yes. They're tracing you anyway. We'll use my bank account. And, I'll tell y'all about them. Maybe we'll sleep in a hotel. They're going to need a hot minute to get ready to send the next team after you. They were really hoping I'd just get you to come back. They aren't going to send Rainer, Jarret, or Anton after you. I don't even know where they are. Rainer got sent out on missions for the company. Jarret was not doing well. It's all coming back. Sort of. They took him away. And Anton... they have special plans I wasn't privy to."

My heart clenched as I heard each of their names. They weren't my mates anymore, but I loved them. The same way I loved the man in front of me.

"Preston, it really might be better for you to go. I have to rescue the whole werewolf world. I have to get revenge on these men. And I'm obviously a mess and a half."

He took my hand across the table. "I'm in love with you, Mac. And despite your emptiness right now, you love me. I can feel it. Hold on? Okay. We're going to get this fixed."

I didn't believe him, but I wanted to.

THREE

I stepped out of the RV and had to block my eyes from the onslaught of the sun. It had been a long time since I'd really spent any time outside the RV during the day. An occasional run into a truck stop was one thing, walking an actual street was something else.

The sun exposed me to more discomfort. I almost turned around and went back inside the RV. Whatever it was, it was secure. For now, anyway.

A smell hit me, taking away my ability to concentrate on anything else. Werewolves. And not the ones I was with. These were new scents that I'd never encountered before. Not just one either, but a whole bunch of them. I staggered backward, and Preston caught me.

"I smell it, too. It's like everywhere. We need to get out of here."

Did we? I wasn't so sure. Everyone on the street had stopped to stare at the three of us. I wasn't getting any hostile scents... just curiosity... and although there were at least twenty souls staring at us, I didn't scent a human among them. How could this be?

The door to a drug store opened, and an older woman strode out. She had gray hair that fell past her waist. With three men trailing after her, she walked straight over to us.

"You're an Omega." She said the words right out there on the street, as if there was no problem saying them whatsoever. My stomach tightened. Being cautious had always been the name of the game.

"You're a werewolf. All of you are. Werewolves who shift," I whispered, I just couldn't help myself. "What is going on here?"

She lifted her eyebrows. "I'm Miranda Howe. And I'll say again, you're an Omega. A sick Omega, but an Omega. You are most welcome here. I can't even believe I'm meeting you. I'd come to think I would never meet another one." She glared at Preston. "She's your mate. Why haven't you taken better care of her?"

"I'm trying. Things are very complicated. We're under attack, basically, and I'm not sure how this place exists, or how y'all are just walking around like this, but we may have brought trouble to you. So, I think the best we can do is get back in our RV and go. Maybe the people after us won't notice."

The woman tilted her head in a very wolf-like way. "What is your name, honey?" She turned to me, not to Preston.

I cleared my throat. "I'm MacKenzie Harper. We have the same initials." That was an asinine thing to say, but my mind was not focused right now. There were too many wolves here, too many eyes on me. My hands burned, and I wasn't sure I could handle a healing. "This is Preston Lejeune."

"Harper," he quickly corrected me. "We're mated.

We're just going through a... thing. Never mind. It's Harper. And that is her brother, Agustin Harper."

Miranda turned to stare at Agustin. "Looks like we'll be family?"

What did that mean? I followed where she indicated with her chin. My brother wasn't listening to us at all. No, his attention was entirely fixated on a werewolf woman down the block. She stared openly right back at him.

"That's my daughter, Laurel. And it looks like she just found her first mate. That makes you family. But I guess we're all family anyway. Behind me, trying not to growl at the idea that their oldest daughter has found a mate, are my own loves. Jesse. Houston. Ryder. To answer your question, we're here because we're here. The last werewolf town I imagine, and we shift because that is what we're meant to do. You have more questions, and you may have brought danger. Well, we'll have to do something about that. Come with me. Get back in your RV and follow me home. We have a lot of things to discuss. Oh, I'm Alpha here. Come on then."

A female? She was Alpha? There were no such things as Alpha females. This was getting stranger and stranger.

Still, I sensed not a lick of danger or ill intent. Preston would do whatever I told him to do in this moment. I needed something to go right. "Let's do what she says."

He pulled me backward. "Okay."

I hoped I wasn't making a huge mistake.

MY BROTHER HAD BECOME a lovesick puppy. One problem, he'd yet to speak to Laurel. Not a word. They stared at each other across Miranda's living room intently, neither of them acting like they could form words. Her fathers were also doing silent staring, but of the less dewy-eyed variety. It was more like death stares.

Miranda shook her head at all of them, and went back to speaking to me after she pushed some chamomile tea my way. I sniffed at it, but Preston picked it up and sipped it before I could make a decision about whether it was okay. He set it down in front of me. "It's fine."

"So, you do know how to protect her." Miranda sat back in her chair.

The living room was beautifully, if sparsely, decorated. I touched the leather couch. It was soft. The whole room was expensive. Whoever this woman was, she wasn't broke, and more power to her. The Lejeune house in New Orleans had looked expensive, too. It was just very contrary to how I'd grown up. I didn't know if I'd ever be really comfortable around high priced things. What if I spilled the chamomile?

"I do." Preston answered. "Or I did. It's complicated. Like I said earlier, we might have brought you trouble."

The woman arched one eyebrow. "I'm not concerned with trouble."

"Men with guns trouble," my brother finally found his tongue.

"We've had men with guns before. We can handle that. They'll never be heard from again."

I sighed. "Some of them might be werewolves who can't help what is happening to them. There are men, rich hunter men, holding them against their wills, mind controlling them. They're doing things they can't help. It's not just a matter of killing them. I have to save them. All of them. And then I have to make those that did this to us pay."

She set down her own tea. "Well, that is more complicated, but nothing we can't handle." She looked over her shoulder, and the one I thought was Houston got to his feet.

He leaned over and kissed Miranda. "On it."

"I took down Preston with a tranq. Then she was able to heal him," Agustin informed them. "And she healed me, too. We were both under their control for a while."

Miranda sighed. "See if we have enough tranqs. If not, send some of the youth to buy some from all the nearby contacts who sell us what we need. Whatever it takes."

I had questions, and much as I sort of enjoyed the way it felt to simply sit here and let Miranda take over, that wasn't going to help anything.

"How are you the Alpha? You're a woman." That might have been the least important question I had, but based on the interactions here, I couldn't help but be struck with it over and over. They deferred to her in the same way someone might defer to Rainer. My brother dropped his eyes like he couldn't quite look at her. I was having trouble watching Preston at all because of all the pain doing so brought me, but I wondered if he was also deferring to her in hierarchy.

I, by contrast, wasn't suffering from the need to look away at all. The longer I had the Omega powers, the more Omega I became.

"Well, I am simply the strongest wolf in town. Naturally, that made me the Alpha. If anyone had a problem with that, they no longer voice it."

I didn't have to have a PhD in wolf talk to know that meant that she'd killed any dissenters. That was what Alphas did if they had anyone oppose them taking over. Individual families had hierarchy, the way that Rainer was for us, and then the pack in general had Alphas. I didn't have the slightest idea who that would be since we had no working pack and I hadn't grown up in one.

"What is this place? How did you avoid the Accords, and what about the Loup problem?"

She sighed. "This place is called Martinsville. Everyone here is a werewolf. We simply find ways to keep humans from settling here. The few who have gone Loup since the death of our Omega disappeared. Ran off. Poor things. No one noticed when we ignored the notices to sign the Accords. We simply never responded. Maybe they forgot we were here. I don't care. No one was coming and taking our wolves."

I wished my own family had done that. "Listen—"

She held up her hand. "We can answer some more questions later. I am happy to. Truly, but now I need to know about you. You're an Omega. You have one mate. He smells stressed."

Did he? I took a breath. Preston's scent was tinged with stress. Why hadn't I noticed? Well, because I'd been pretty preoccupied with a lot lately, and I wasn't even sure I wanted to notice. Noticing hurt.

"We've been through a lot. I'm afraid it's hard to explain all of it, but we were mated. Then these very rich former hunters took them away. Corporations? Or something? My mating marks went away. And now we're all in this situation."

Preston shook his head. "My mark is just fine." He pulled down his shirt just a bit to show that the mark was still there.

"And yours went away?" Miranda studied me.

Preston put his face in his hands and rubbed his hands over the front of his features like they hurt him. "Mates who survive each other after death keep their marks. I can't explain it, and you're right. She's sick. I can't fix it. I've never missed my brothers more than I do now, and I went years without thinking about the fact that I never saw them." He paused. "Why am I telling you all this?"

Across the room, Laurel laughed. "Everyone tells her things. It's part of being the Alpha."

Miranda nodded. "It's okay. I understand better now. Yes, your mate, the first Omega born in this generation is sick. I'm afraid she might be dying."

I jolted. "What?"

With a sharp tug, Preston pulled me against him. "She's not dying."

"Well, not if I can help it." She rose. "My sister was our Omega. She succumbed when all the Omegas did. I need to hear more about this mind control. But not right now. There'll be no point in any of this if you perish in the night."

Preston blocked her when she would have walked from the room. "You didn't blink about the marks vanishing. I've never heard anything like this before."

"I know many things Mr. Harper. Yes, it's very unusual, but it's an Omega thing. I'm afraid it comes from extreme anger."

He nodded fast. "I can scent that. I just have to figure out how to get her to forgive me."

I'd had enough. "I'm not angry at you. I'm angry at me. Okay? Horribly. Like I can't breathe angry, so everyone just stop. Please, just stop."

Well, there, I'd said it. The words were out there. I couldn't take them back.

Miranda pointed up the stairs. "Take the third room on the left. It's very private. I'm going to stay down here and get to know your brother a little better, and see that Laurel does, too. You two have much to speak about."

We did. I just didn't know how to do any of it.

THE VIEW from the bedroom was lovely. There was green landscape everywhere with an occasional house here and there. I didn't know how far the pack land went. That was a question for later. I was avoiding looking at Preston.

Finally, I turned, facing him. He'd not moved from the door since I crossed the room.

His eyes were wolf. Yes, he was waiting for me to be honest with him, and he deserved it. "I never blamed you for what happened. I need to be clear about that. Nothing was your fault." I swallowed. "It was all my fault."

Preston furrowed his brow. "How do you figure that? This has been going on since before you were born."

"Because I'm a terrible Omega. I... The truth is that I should have been able to prevent what happened. I never fixed Anton. I never had any inclination that I should." My voice cracked. It was hard to utter the reality eating me up from the inside. The failure never gave me a moment's rest from its aching presence, though my empty tried to eat them away, dissolve them, destroy them. "Your mother even told me."

He reached for me, and I let him hold me. I'd never expected to have his arms around me again. All I wanted to do was roll around and get lost in the strong power that was Preston. Yet, the comfort wouldn't fix the truth. I kept speaking. "She told me. They'd broken him, and there I was like some kind of expert... insisting he wasn't broken. That there was nothing wrong with him. I made a whole fucking speech. She's his mother, and she knew. I dismissed your mother like she was clueless because I judged her."

I pulled away to look at him. "Preston, my powers never turned on. They never alerted me. I never considered testing to see if there was even something I could find. Why? Because I cleared a couple of Loups? I am an Omega. A terrible one. You told me so yourself."

He shook his head. "Mac, you know I didn't mean that—"

I interrupted him. "And I'm so angry. I'm so fucking angry at myself. I'm empty inside. I deserve to be. So, I didn't understand it or know what it was, but I suppose it makes sense. I ended the mating. I'm saving you from me."

He rubbed my cheeks with his thumbs. I hadn't realized I'd been weeping. "Ssshh." He kissed my tears. "Listen to me, Mac. Please listen very closely." His voice was a whisper in my ears. "What happened to Anton happened when he was very, very young. I don't know that you could have known. I think it was deeply entrenched in him, so small and in there so deeply, you'd have... I don't know... to have been doing this a lot longer than you were to know."

"Pres." I sucked in a sob. "Stop letting me off the hook."

"That's not what I'm doing. And it's my turn to talk. Let me." He kissed my temple. "There's one more thing to this... I can assure you that my mother did not have some great insight that you ignored. Mac, she kept him away from the world. Homeschooled him so no one could make her teach him sign language or any other useful tool. She just kept acting like something was going to fix itself. And my fathers let her, because they didn't have a clue about what to do with her grief and her blaming herself. Which she absolutely needed to do, considering she left my little brothers alone, unsupervised, in the house. Yes, she was tricked into doing it, but at the end of the day, it was a choice she made.

But at some point, you suck up your guilt, and you get on with not making things worse."

I put my hands on his chest. It was everything I could do not to wrap my arms around his neck and never let go. "Preston, I'm not interested in trashing your mother."

"My turn. If she was talking about him being broken, then she was talking about his voice. End of story. As for the rest of it? You can't take you away from us. We need you. We chose this."

I wasn't making him understand. "You don't know that. We all shifted, and we liked the scent and—"

"No." Preston's voice was low and dead serious. "Don't you know how mating works?"

"I... I thought that I did."

He took my hand and led me to the bed. I stopped on the edge of it. I didn't know if I could do this, if I could let the intimacy of what lying there with him would do to me. He let go of my hand and sat, waiting a bit before he did anything at all.

The bed was white and soft looking. Preston, on the edge of it, patted the spot next to him for me to sit down. Could I be brave? Finally, I made myself move to join him. My knees practically gave out in relief. My head hurt, and the constant pain in my body was a dull throb. Dying. Was that why I hurt so much?

"The mating takes place so fast that we aren't fully conscious of it until it hits all at once, the way it did with your brother on the street. But it goes like this. The female knows what she needs, what kind of wolf she needs. I don't know if it's strength, if it's power, if it's fertility. I imagine every werewolf has a different desire, or craving in a mate. But the female knows. She even knows just how many she's going to need. And then she scents the male. If he meets her requirements, she sends out a psychic wolf signal to the male. He takes a look and decides if that's what he wants, if he's interested in bonding to her wolf." He tugged on the end of my hair. "And he says yes. Then we realize it. That fast." He snapped his fingers. "They've already had that conversation. So let me assure you, Omega-of-mine, that I *decided*. I knew what I was getting, and I said fuck yes. It's not some spiritual, otherworldly, fated mate thing. It's chemistry. It's choice."

I shook my head. "You know that you are basically spitting on years and years of werewolf understanding by putting it like that."

"Yeah, well, fuck it. I know the truth. I used to listen to the males I grew up with talk about this. That's how it works. I chose this. I want this. My brothers do, too. You're not a bad Omega. You're a *new* Omega, and it seems maybe a very, very sick Omega. Please, let me help you. I love you. You keep saving me. My turn."

He implored me with his gaze. I didn't have to read his thoughts like I did his brother, but that didn't mean I couldn't. Preston meant every word that he said.

"Pres, I'm not sure I could survive losing another mark."

My love took my hands in his, kissing my knuckles. "Don't get so angry that you lose them again. Talk to me. I'm not going anywhere. Whatever they did to Anton... it connected to us on the same psychic level that you did when we decided we were going to be mates. The family level. But you fixed it. Changed the frequency. Cleared it out."

How could he be sure of any of this? "Preston, we don't know that was how it worked."

"I do. I'm the one who went through it. I can feel the disconnect. I can... I know the difference. Come on. You need to rest, and then we'll go down and tell these people everything I know. See if we can help keep them safe, and see if they can help us undo what has happened. Not just to us, but to everyone."

I rubbed my fingers over the stubble on his cheeks, loving the bite of it on my fingertips. "I am exhausted. But I don't want to sleep."

He sucked in his breath. "What do you want to do?"

I'd been brave sitting next to him. Could I do it again? "I want you to give me back my mark."

He gave me such a beautiful smile, that it stilled my heart for the utter gorgeousness of it. "I'd love to give you back your mark."

Preston kissed me gently, our lips barely brushing. I needed closer. I needed whatever it took to have him back. The pain didn't matter. I'd spent so much time ignoring it. I could certainly do so now, particularly when my wolf pushed into my eyes, taking control, changing the way colors looked, the way light reverberated. Making everything sharper. The first time she'd done that in a month.

He halted kissing me to stroke my face. His own eyes were still wolf. We stared at each other like that. "We picked each other."

I wanted to believe what he seemed so sure of. How did any of us really know anything about any of this? I loved the romanticism of thinking we'd had a silent conversation that we'd not been conscious of, and then decided that we perfectly fit. He took my hand and placed it on the hardness bulging in his pants. "Do you feel what you do to me? A month is too long to not have been in your warmth. I love you."

I shifted, then straddled his lap. We were face-to-face, breathing hard, and we'd hardly begun. "In the beginning, some nights, I tried to picture you. Tried to touch myself thinking of you, but it wasn't the same. I couldn't get there."

He kissed the end of my nose, both of my eyes. "I'm going to take such good care of you. I'm going to make you come and come again."

Experience told me he would. He rolled us over until he was on top of me on the bed. My empty tried to surge out, and I pushed it back down. I hoped doing this would be the first step to eliminating the emptiness. Like a parasite, it didn't want to be gotten rid of. I was working on bravery. Could I fix my thinking? Could I make this happen? Was I strong enough to push through the things that had been torturing me?

I was in charge of what I let control my life.

I wanted Preston. That was it. He was my mate.

He pulled off my shorts, throwing them aside. Preston ran his hands up my legs, stopping right below my underwear. With one finger, he dragged them down my legs, and they vanished in the same direction as my shorts. Preston leaned over, breathing in by my pussy. He lifted his gaze to meet mine and smiled. "There is nothing like the way that you smell."

I grinned back at him. "Preston. What are you doing down there?"

He pressed his tongue against me, finding my clit first. Preston swirled his tongue over my clit, and I gasped. The sound quickly changed to a moan. I closed my eyes and gripped onto the bed. We should probably have been quiet, but I wasn't sure I was capable of it.

He left my clit and pressed his tongue deep inside of me. I shuddered. Oh, Preston had a magic tongue. I was going to be a quivering mess, and I couldn't get there fast enough. I drew my knees up, closer to my chest, trying to draw him deeper, needing so much more. He stopped me, holding onto my leg. Over and over, he found my rhythm, and soon I was coming hard. Goosebumps broke out on my body, colors passed through my eyes. Still, even as I came, it wasn't enough.

I panted. I needed him but not just like that. Preston seemed to understand. I opened my eyes, and we undressed each other the rest of the way without words. I ran my hands over my mark on him a second before he took one of my nipples in his mouth. I wrapped my legs around his waist. We rocked against each other, over and over again. I didn't need any more warm up, but I truly didn't want to rush a moment of this.

Moments were precious, few and far between.

Eventually, he slowed and eased away enough so I could reach his cock. I stroked him, and now it was his turn to moan. This was such a gift. Getting to touch him. I wouldn't take it for granted. His noises increased in volume. Preston released my breast, but only so he could make love to my mouth. Our tongues danced together as he positioned himself where he could enter me.

I nodded at him. Yes, I wanted this. Him. A reconnection.

Preston pushed inside of me. I arched my back, loving how he filled me. It was all I could think about as he moved in and out of me. I raised my hips to meet his thrusts. I loved this. I. Loved. This. He was mine.

I might not have been everything I should be, but he loved me anyway.

He wanted this. He'd chosen this, or at least he thought he had, and that was enough for me. It didn't take long, and as the bed squeaked beneath us, I saw his fangs. Yes, he was going to bite me. Right in his spot.

"Now," I begged him, and he didn't let me down. While I came like a cascade, I couldn't stop even if I'd wanted to, Preston marked me, and it was such a fucking relief. I would never let him go again. That was my mark. I was keeping it. And him.

FOUR

I lay in the pool made by the afternoon sun, bathing the room in a surreal light, like we were out of time somehow. My forehead was pressed against Preston's, and we breathed, sharing air like we had nothing exciting to do in the world at all.

"You should sleep," he told me for the third time.

"My pain has lessened a little bit," I answered him. "Kind of a dull ache I could probably sleep through but, Pres, I don't sleep."

"Why not?"

I sighed. "It sounds nuts, but I swear werewolves are reaching out to me psychically in my sleep, and it's so stressful, I wake up."

He furrowed his brow. "Why is it stressful?"

"They ask for me to heal them. The last one was in California. I can't help them."

Preston leaned up on his arm. "Damn."

"Yep. It's physically painful, to the point that it drags my exhausted mind back to wakefulness as if it's the only way to escape their need. It's just awful. Honestly, Preston, I'm not sure how much longer I can do this."

He sighed before he kissed my nose. "We're going to figure this out. I'll drug you if it comes to that."

"With what? The tranq was fully dosed, and it barely knocked you out an hour. We're werewolves, we run through those meds like they're nothing at all."

Preston didn't have an easy answer, but I suspected he mulled this problem over in his mind. Maybe he'd come up with an answer my brother and I hadn't.

"Not that I'm complaining," he said, a smirk tilting the corners of his mouth. "But why did you decide to take me back? What made you decide to?"

I almost made a joke about liking his hair better without the tips, but this was a serious moment, it deserved that kind of respect. I smiled at him. "I guess I needed to hear you tell me that... that you didn't blame me, and that it wasn't my fault. I guess I couldn't fathom *having* you back without it."

Preston kissed my lips gently.

"Try to go to sleep now. You said your pain is easing. Maybe the sleep will come more easily now. You were sleeping just fine when you were with us."

I chewed on my bottom lip. It was sore from all the kissing we'd been doing. I couldn't say I particularly minded. "The first few days before we really cemented us, I did have nightmares—memories, really—of my time with the hunters in the labs."

"And then we got together, and it cooled off. Maybe that'll happen again."

I hoped he was right. The last thing I wanted to do was sleep. But my mind was so tired, I could barely function. We had to find everyone, rescue my other guys, and every other wolf that had been taken by these psychopaths. I couldn't do any of that if I couldn't think. Plus, Miranda thought I was dying. I had a feeling that had more to do with the lack of sleep than the pain. How much longer could I go?

"Can we stay like this?" I stared up at his strong jawline. "Or do you have to go do things?"

He opened his arms. "This is all I want to do, Mac. Take care of you. That's what I want more than anything. Get you well, and then we'll figure things out."

I pressed my head against his chest to hear his heartbeat. Preston was here. I'd managed to cure him. If I could do that, then there was hope to all of this. He wrapped his arm around me, not objecting to having the full weight of my body trapping his other arm.

I closed my eyes, not expecting to sleep.

But the world drifted away.

"WHERE ARE YOU, OMEGA?" The man crawled on the ground toward me. "I'm turning into a Loup. I'm trying so hard not to, but I can't control it. Please. Please. Please. Help me."

I swallowed. My hands burned with the need to help him but this wasn't real. I wouldn't be able to do a thing.

I bent over to touch his head. "Where are you?"

He lifted his head to look at me with such hope in his eyes it broke my heart. "I'm in Florida."

I wasn't there.

I WOKE UP WITH A GASP, my heart racing. Preston

lifted his head to stare at me. "Well, that wasn't long enough at all."

I tried to swallow as my body shook. "How long?"

He rubbed my temple with his thumb. "About thirty-two minutes. Not long enough at all."

I sat up. "Yeah... well, unless we can hightail it to Florida, I can't help that man. And I can't sleep through his pain."

"Anything I can do?" He kissed me. "I wasn't being creepy or anything watching you sleep. I tried to brainstorm ideas, but I've got nothing other than letting you sleep and getting you fed."

I shook my head. "Maybe it's time for you to tell everyone what you remember, so I can see if it helps find the others."

He nodded. "Let's go find Miranda."

Who needed sleep? Apparently, it didn't matter if I did, the need of every wolf in the country wouldn't allow it.

WE SAT around Miranda's table. My hands burned, and I sipped tea. She seemed very dedicated to serving it to me.

"My sister loved it." She patted my arm. "Found it calming."

I didn't. But I smiled because it was so nice of her. My brother sat in the corner, very close to Laurel. They whispered to each other, and I smiled. Clearly, in our hour or so upstairs they'd worked out their shyness with each other. My brother, a mated wolf—I wouldn't have imagined it.

"So, we thought it might be helpful for you to hear what I know." Preston cleared his throat. "Unless you'd prefer not."

Miranda's mates came into the room, joining her, until they'd taken up every other seat at the table. She patted the table, to reclaim Preston's attention. "Talk."

It was a tribute to her power that Preston did it without blinking. He listened to Rainer, but not quite as quickly. That was okay. I liked how powerful Rainer was. I didn't want a change up in that structure.

"My understanding from the things Brennan said was that there were multiple families involved in this, like some kind of hunters turned corporation that really just wanted to kill us all. I only ever heard one name. The doctors who poked at me with needles, and eventually ordered me to come try and capture you, kept talking about Ross Morgan. He seemed to be in charge of us. Oh, they'd say, Mr. Morgan is coming. Or do you know Ross? I wish I could give you more information, but it wasn't like I roamed freely around. It's more like I heard things—through the fog of my consciousness—when they spoke in front of me. I was vaguely aware of others. When they took Jarret away because he wasn't, according to them, doing well, I knew that happened. But I don't know what that meant, or where he went. And I never saw Rainer or Anton at all."

"Anton Lejeune." Laurel hopped to her feet and came over. She was a pretty girl with kind eyes. I liked how she smelled fresh and unassuming. I liked it even more how my brother couldn't take his gaze from her. "The author?"

Preston nodded. "That's him. That's the little brother."

"Oh, I love his books. I had no idea he was a werewolf. I have all of them on my ereader."

My stomach clenched. "I still haven't read him."

"You totally need to." She rushed out of the room and came back with her tablet. "Please use this. Read him. I am in... well, when I meet him, I'm going to fangirl him."

I loved that term. "I've never had a sister. It'll be really nice to have you in the family."

Her smile was huge as she wrapped me in a tight embrace. Apparently, she was a hugger. I made note in my mind. I'd have to get used to it, but I wouldn't hurt this girl for anything in the world. She was open, kind, and my powers didn't want to fix her at all. That had been a problem with Anton, but for now I'd call it a win.

If she turned out to have some horrible issue that I should have fixed and didn't, I was going to be pretty pissed at these Omega powers.

Her mother sighed. "It seems my entire pack wants you to help them. Are you willing?"

I gaped at her. "Is there a choice? My powers hurt. If I don't use them, they hurt worse. Yes, I'll fix them." I got to my feet. "How about I start with you?"

Her eyes widened. "Me? You're feeling like you need to fix me?"

Why did she sound so surprised? "Yes. Probably smart to begin with you. Healthy Alpha, healthy pack." Not like I'd know. When had I ever had a pack? Still, she didn't object or disagree.

I scooted my chair closer to hers and took her hand in mine. I closed my eyes. The trouble with my Omega ability was I never knew exactly how I was going to have to use it. Did I need to shift? I had no idea. Sometimes I did, sometimes I didn't. There was neither rhyme nor reason I'd stumbled over as to why I had to do things sometimes and not others. What in the ever-loving fuck was I supposed to do to differentiate one situation from another?

Images flowed into my head. I blinked. Well, that was a first. It took me a second to realize that I wasn't so much seeing as I smelled them. I smiled. There was ease to this. I could scent who she was, and my mind created images for it. What an amazing feeling. Yes, this woman was the real deal. She cared about her pack, she ran things as kindly as she could, everyone respected her. I could trust this woman to have the best possible interests of the werewolves around her. She was a survivor, and she kept her people afloat, despite how hard things had gotten.

I sent her healing energy. It wasn't hard. This must have been what it was like when things were normal for werewolves. An Alpha could simply reach out to an Omega and have an easy healing at the kitchen table. The burning in my hands lessened, petering out one second after another. I pulled away. My energy level was pretty okay. She hadn't drained me. It was a nice, pleasant encounter. I didn't expect all of my Omega jobs to be like that, but it was nice to know that it simply could be.

I leaned back in my chair. "Who's next?"

The Alpha smiled at me. "Oh, no one. You're done for the night. Tomorrow, maybe you'll do a few more. We won't be draining you to death."

I shrugged. "I'm not sure tomorrow will make a difference, and who knows what—"

"Ma'am." A wolf entered the room. He bowed his head, avoiding eye contact with the Alpha. "They're here, and we're handling it."

All three of Miranda's mates rose and exited. My brother and Preston both leaped to their feet. "What's going on?" Preston ran to the window, his eyes wolf.

"They've sent their gunmen." She smiled but didn't rise. "It's being handled."

My breath caught. "Miranda, some of those gunmen are human, and some of them are bound to be wolves who can't help what they are doing."

She tapped her nose. "It's a good thing we're wolves, then. Don't worry. No wolves will be hurt on my watch. Not when they've been hurt by some humans." She said that last word like it tasted badly on her tongue. "We have the tranqs. That was a great idea."

I nodded toward my brother. "That was Agustin's idea."

"Looks like my daughter made a good choice." She smiled like that didn't surprise her. "Smart one, Laurel."

Preston cleared his throat. "We're not cowards. We would help with this."

"Well, of course you would. I can smell that about you. But you aren't my pack. If you want to leave your swamp and swear allegiance to me, to take your Omega and be mine, you can fight with us. I assume her brother will do so. If not, we need to have a different conversation. But I digress. Is that what you want, Preston? Because we don't let visitors fight with us."

And there was the Alpha toughness I'd smelled when I cleared her of pain. A muscle ticked in Preston's jaw. "I will always do what Mac wants, unless it's bad for her. But no, I don't intend to leave my swamp. We come from that swamp. All of us. At some point your family did, too."

She waved her hand. "Oh, yes we did. And if we'd stayed, we'd be as destroyed as the rest of you. I knew you would say no. Much as I would love to keep your Omega here." She rose just as the sound of gunfire echoed in the distance. I jumped, but Miranda stayed steady. "All is fine. It's all expected." She scented the air and smiled. "Going just as we would want."

I looked around. She could tell that from sniffing the air? My own scenting ability was quite different. It was more about how people felt... not what they were doing.

I walked over to Preston and held onto his arm, needing

the contact in this moment. My brother had put Laurel behind him and in front of the wall so that no one could get near them.

"You don't go fight with them?" Wasn't that something an Alpha would do?

"They don't let me. Alphas are to be kept safe. I hate sending others to battle, and if it were going badly, I would go help. But we're winning."

Laurel laughed. "This is a longstanding fight. My mother mated the three best fighters in the pack. They feel they represent her well enough."

"I used to battle quite well before I was a mated were-wolf." She shook her head. "Back when we had to fight for resources in that swamp of yours."

I had questions about that, but I didn't have time to ask them before the smell of a dozen or so werewolves approaching the house hit me hard. I stepped back as they dragged five unconscious werewolves into the living room.

"Put them on the couches. In this room, and the den. Did you lose any wolves?"

Houston grunted, which I guessed meant no as he kept speaking. "Nope. Only humans, and they seemed rather shocked. Came at us like we didn't know how to fight."

"That's because most of us don't." My brother and I were already moving as he spoke. One of the five knocked out wolves was our oldest brother Isaac. We both stared down at him. He was alive, but he looked different than the last time I'd seen him. Isaac had never been a bulky guy; he was more studious and tended to spend his free time watching movies, not going to the gym. Of course, he'd never had the ability to shift before. So maybe he'd just put on muscle. Or maybe they'd been forcing him to get bigger.

Agustin turned to me. "You got this. I know you do. For all of them."

I looked over my shoulder at Miranda. She was remarkably good at knowing things that weren't said to her, but just in case she didn't know, I wanted to make sure she knew who this was. "This is our oldest brother."

Miranda made a noise in the back of her throat that was something like hmm. "They send your brothers to kill you. Your mate to kill you. No wonder you can't sleep, Omega."

I smiled at her. "Kidnap or kill me. Don't forget the possibility of torture. But I'm still here. So far, it's MacKenzie-3, crazy humans-0." I hadn't even noticed when my hands started to burn. It was such a common feeling for me now. "Let's get these guys feeling better before they wake up."

Miranda gaped at me. "Five? You're going to do five right now? My sister couldn't have managed that, and she wasn't as drained as you."

I shook my head. "All five... They're not spending another night like this."

Preston leaned over and whispered in my ear. "If only you were ever really as confident as you pretend to be. You are remarkable, and I love you."

I smiled at him. "I love you, too. We have to leave after this. I know this pack is strong, but I won't be the reason they are destroyed. The humans will send bigger forces the next time."

Preston nodded. "Yep."

I was glad we were on the same page. These were kind werewolves. They deserved better than to be caught up in my mess. They'd managed to hide in plain sight all of these years. I was going to see to it that they got to keep doing so.

I smiled at Preston. "Don't let me fall."

"Never."

He meant it, but we both knew that sometimes I was going to, and there wasn't a thing he could do about it. Of course, his answer was as fantastical as my asking the question in the first place.

I dug deep. It was going to be a long day.

I HAD AN APPETITE, which was a nice change. Despite the desperate ache in every limb of my body, I was able to eat dinner before I climbed into bed. Preston put his head on my shoulder. "They're all going to be fine."

His tired pushed against my own. "You should sleep."

"You don't. I will when you do."

I shook my head. "Honey, whatever is allowing me to keep going, it's Omega-related. You need to sleep, so that you're there if I lose it. Okay? I'll read. I'm not going to do anything or rescue anyone else, unless it's an outright emergency. I have Anton's books to get through. Maybe I'll doze off. We both know it'll be about half an hour. You should get a full night's rest right here next to me, where I know you can protect me if something goes wrong."

He lifted his eyebrows. "Totally manipulating me with that last part there. I know you too well. You aren't giving two seconds of a thought about needing to be protected. Even Miranda doesn't know what to do with the fact that you won't stop."

That was probably true. "Agustin will stay here when we go. He'll try not to, because he feels obligated, but he needs to be with Laurel now."

Preston nodded. "True."

"And Isaac should stay, too. I don't even know if he'll

want to come, but if he makes any moves to do so, we need to make him stay. He needs to rest. You and I will get in the RV and go wherever we are headed next."

He lifted his head to look at me. I stared forward, but his gaze moved over me as though he touched me with the tips of his fingertips. "We could go home. Back to the swamp. They know where we are, and they are tracking us, so maybe we should just go back home."

I sucked in a breath. The last time I had been there, Kevin died and the guys were taken. But he was right. That wasn't any more dangerous than anywhere else, and we were fooling ourselves thinking we could be safe staying on the move. "All right. Yes. Let's go home."

He kissed my cheek. "I'm going to sleep so I can drive us straight there tomorrow. I'll drive all night if I need to. I love you."

It was cozy being wrapped up against him, and Preston's presence did seem to ease some of my ache. My empty was still there, just less likely to form a lasso and try to strangle me and everyone else around me. It was more like a constant throbbing that I could somewhat ignore if I needed to. I'd love it to go away, but beggars couldn't be choosers.

I read Anton's book, the low illumination from Laurel's ereader enough that I could enjoy the way my youngest mate used words. He was detail-oriented and built a world where aliens had come to earth to be hidden. Four brothers. They were in deep trouble if they were found. I chewed on my bottom lip, flipping through the pages. Some of this had to have been pulled from real life.

The characters had to have been based on Rainer, Preston, Jarret, and Anton himself. Hunters were after them. No one was mute, but they all felt misunderstood, unheard, they were looking for something and trying to avoid being science experiments. Not all of it was from his real life. I didn't think. Purple laser arrays and five-legged aliens were probably all fictional. But I could see why readers liked this.

It really sucked me in.

I was halfway through the book when they were all caught. I blinked. The hunters were given viewpoints as they scurried off with the heroes, their own voices halting in the storyline as they became prisoners.

I sat up straighter, and Preston started to snore, his head moving into a strange position on the pillow. Goosebumps broke out on my arms. There was description in this that seemed almost real. Locations of places where the alien hunters sent people for various activities. Where they went for torture. Where they went for mind control. Where they went to be experimented on. To be held captive.

This didn't seem so fictional anymore. This felt more like Anton had left the world—had left *me*—a message.

"Preston..." My voice was scratchy from disuse. "I need you to wake up."

His eyes opened instantly, and he sat up. "What's wrong, Mac? Talk to me. What do you need?"

I breathed in through my nose to stop the excitement from causing me to hyperventilate. "I need you to believe me, when what I have to say is crazy."

He turned on the light. "Okay."

I held up the ereader. "I think Anton told us where to go. I think he told us where everyone is."

Preston opened and closed his mouth. "How did he do that?"

"In his book. This one. With the aliens. Detention centers all over the place. He knew where they were."

Preston scrunched up his face, even as he took the ereader from my hand. "Why would he do that? If he'd known something like that, why wouldn't he have just told us? I mean the man was smart, but he wasn't some kind of future predicting psychic. And he'd not have hidden it. Fuck, he'd tell us. He'd want to be rescued."

Yes, all of that made sense. They were good arguments. But I knew just what had happened. Maybe I was nuts, but I'd never felt saner in my life. "What if he didn't know that he knew? What if he just overheard things like you did? People coming in and out of the room. He heard things."

"Mac, he was a baby when they took him. How could he even remember? Sure, not an infant. A toddler, but same difference. Again, he was smart, but not that smart."

I took Preston's hand. This part was hard. "What if that was not the only time they took him, Pres? What if they have periodically had your brother on and off this whole time? Would you know?" I leveled him a glare. "Would he?"

Preston swallowed, the realization of what I'd said crossing his gaze. Yes, he felt it now too—the utter terror mixed with the idea that there might be answers to be found. This was really happening. "Fuck."

FIVE

Three in the morning, and everyone in the house was awake, taking notes on Anton's book like it had suddenly become a textbook. If I was wrong about this, I was going to lose all credibility, and deservedly so. I had a theory, and I'd brought everyone into it. I chewed on my lips. The great Omega detective I was not.

Miranda left and came back with a map she laid flat on the dining room table in front of us. The wolves I'd helped were starting to wake up, and my brother Isaac joined us to help after he ate something. He was groggy. All of the saved wolves were, and I couldn't blame them. They'd been through hell, and they didn't even remember getting here. Laurel had immediately felt the mate connection with a male named Lamont Feuerstein, who hailed from the Pacific Northwest. He was thrilled, and so far, he got along with Agustin. The poor man had quite a shock when he learned it had been two years since he'd been taken. Two years of his life—just gone.

I hated these fuckers who had done this to all of us. But

there would be time for me to have all kinds of feelings about it later. For now, I had to try to decipher Anton's book like it was code, and that was easier said than done.

How he described things wasn't necessarily how someone else would. We were pretty sure the center that held the aliens in his first book, where they were held while their captors decided what to do with them, had been in North Carolina. The description of the Outer Banks with horses running on the beach seemed pretty clear. That was where Gus had found me, and we knew that place had been destroyed. They weren't there now.

So, what did that mean?

Preston tapped Atlanta on the map. "Look, we have to assume that the place where they take the ones who aren't doing well to determine if they should be... *put down*... is where Jarret is. Where any of them in that situation are. I'm going to say Atlanta. Anton loves football. We're from Louisiana. We live and die for the Black and Gold. The Saints. He called it the place of the hated black bird. That's got to be the Falcons. We play in the same division. It's not a pretty rivalry."

I shivered. Jarret had to be okay. I couldn't... well, I wouldn't allow myself to think otherwise. I was beyond relieved Preston had been able to translate the falcon reference to football. "And then, there is the control center where the wolves they're going to send out for various things are housed and trained. That's where I must have been, where Isaac, Rainer, maybe Anton all are. He's talking about dolphins. If I take the same reference, assume he's still talking about football, then we're heading to Miami."

Isaac shook his head. "I think that is right, but there are other places. Weigh stations. Cowboys. I'm going to go with Dallas. He moves on from the football. Apples. New York. We really need to spread out and do this. The problem being that my sister has to clear everyone. There is no one else to help. And she can't be in at least five places at once."

"No, but I'm going to Atlanta and Miami. My mates are, hopefully, there. Then I'm going home. I'm not placing Miranda's pack in any more danger by staying here."

The Alpha shook her head. "They'll be gunning for us anyway, but I do understand your desire to go home. We are pack animals. Your small pack belongs there. I'll help you. We'll go, and if I have your permission, we'll get your house set up with cages. We'll hold who we can, get tracking devices out of them, and wait for you to come back. Our other teams can get who they can from these places and go to your home with them."

Preston lifted his eyebrows. "I can promise you, Alpha, you're always welcome in our homes."

"Thank you." She cleared her throat. "I hate to disagree, Omega, but I don't think you can afford to go to Atlanta and Miami. Once you hit one, they could uproot and go elsewhere. You need to do one and trust the other groups to take care of your mates, if they're in the other place." She took my hand. "Plus, we can't storm the cities. They're huge places. We have great noses, but the reason they stay either entirely remote or go to big cities, has to be the ability to hide in plain sight."

She was right. I dropped in my seat. "What are we going to do? I'll never forget that sick, metallic smell that comes off all of the wolves. But I have to be close to it to get it. I imagine even as awful as it is, the scent could be masked in a city.

"Don't fret. I have an idea. It might be hard, but maybe

you can do it. Do you have dreams of other wolves? Who need you?"

I lifted my head. "All the time. It's why I can't sleep. They hurt."

She nodded. "Yes, of course they do. And that won't stop. I'm sorry. You'll figure out how to rest when you have your mates back. I hope. But you can connect to those who need you." She widened her eyes, and even though I was mostly immune these days to pack hierarchy, I almost lowered mine. The woman was seriously powerful.

"That would make great sense if I had any control over who I see. It's random. I can't pick and choose. It could be years before I accidentally stumble on someone we need."

She held my gaze, and I forced myself to endure it. Goosebumps broke out on my arms. "Listen to me, MacKenzie Harper, this is entirely unfair what is being asked of you. You're too new, too young, too untrained. There is no one to really help you except me, and all I have are anecdotal memories told to me from my sister, whose experience may not be your own. But you have to push yourself, and that's asking even more of you, considering you're already at your edge. You can connect with people of your choice. This is an Omega connection with all were-wolves. My sister was once able to find someone she needed to help in another country, simply by reaching out every night while she slept."

"It's so strange she's the Omega." Isaac looked at Agustin.

"You'll get used to it, and you have no idea how much weirder it can get than this." Agustin shook his head.

Miranda ignored my family. "Try."

What I wouldn't give for someone to teach me how to do this. "I guess I'd better try to go to bed."

I met Preston's gaze. This wasn't going to be easy.

"I get kidnapped, mind messed with. And when I come back to myself, it's in a strange alternative reality where my sister is the Omega, mated to the Lejeunes, and my brother has somehow mated with the daughter of a female Alpha." Isaac rubbed his face. "Things certainly took an unexpected turn."

"Relax, Isaac." I patted his shoulder. "I'm sure you're going to get to have tons of fun, too."

He snorted. I did love my family. We'd lived a really quiet life. Isaac was right. I'd never have predicted this.

"I'VE NEVER HAD pressure to go to sleep before. I mean, I guess there's always pressure in the sense that you have to go to sleep sometimes in a hurry, if you don't want to be tired the next day. But not... not like this."

Preston rubbed my back. "I'm going to be up when you are. So you'll wake up, and you'll tell me, and you'll try again. We'll just keep at it until we get somewhere."

I appreciated the "we," but it was just me who had to do this. Not that I disputed him. Pres was really trying hard here.

I sighed. "Whining doesn't help, but the idea of this constant in and out of sleep makes me feel sick to my stomach. I don't have a choice, so what will be will be. I'd love some kind of direction. Is there a way to focus my brain? Should I think about them?"

Preston shook his head. "No idea. It can't hurt. Okay, let's try to think about what my brothers would say if they were here. Rainer would tell you that it would be fine, whatever happened. Jarret would say he believed in you. That you are a miracle, and that you can do anything. And Anton... he would tell you that you were his heart, and just to keep going, because you'd get through this and get it done."

Sadness threatened to overwhelm me, and my empty swirled to life. "I miss them."

It didn't help to say it aloud. Maybe it should have, but it didn't. Instead, it just widened the raw loss, made the empty even bigger, as though talking about them gave it permission to come out and play.

He nodded before he kissed the end of my nose. "I do, too. And there was a time I'd never have believed that. When we fell apart, we did so big time. Rainer and I were close, and then he got sent away. I was so angry at him for not fighting back against the BS charges they'd shoved at him. I just... I retreated. Started the business. Decided I was done with all of them. Why bother to be a family, when they didn't want to be one? Then you came." He cupped my cheek, and some of that empty pulled back, tightening instead of expanding. "You made us a family again. I ache for them. You're not alone, Mac."

I wrapped my arms around his neck and held on. "Don't let me go while I sleep, okay? I know it's a lot to ask. You have to be exhausted, too. I need you, Preston. I love you, and I can't do this without you."

"My mate." He kissed both my cheeks, his eyes going wolf. "I'll be here for you every long second of this."

I WENT to sleep thinking of Jarret. Preston said he wasn't doing well. That meant I had to get to him first, before the unthinkable happened. Unfortunately, it wasn't Jarret I saw when I opened my eyes in dreamland.

A man stood in front of me, shivering. He wasn't tall; maybe my own height, and he had hair graying at his temples. He shook wildly and stared at me. "Omega? Are you an Omega?"

I nodded. He was a wolf in trouble. "I am. I'm sorry. I'm not here to help you. I wish that I was."

"This is a terrible place." He shook again. "I don't feel right. And there are voices in my head. Everyone here is in bad shape."

My head stuttered. Okay. I'd wanted to get to Jarret, and this wasn't him, but maybe I'd come to the right place. "Did someone take you and bring you here?"

The poor man blinked rapidly. "I think so, but it's so confusing. Yes, that's what happened."

I strode toward him. If I could have touched him, if I could have healed him, I would have done so. "Are there others there with you?"

He spoke fast. "Yes. They're trying to fix us. To inject us with drugs. To... I'm not sure. It hurts, Omega."

"I know it does." I swallowed. "I am so sorry about that. I need you to look around. Is there a window? Can you see outside? Is there anything that could tell me where you are?"

He shook his head. "I can't see anything in here, and it always feels like I'm in a fog."

That was pretty universal for the wolves who went through this. Pea soup. "I know."

"But on the way in, I heard things. The drivers were talking. A river. Started with a C. And a highway 285. I'm sorry, not more than that."

If I could have hugged him, I would have. "That's huge. What is your name?"

He smiled at me. "Richard Green. You think you can come here?"

"I'm going to do my best. To get to you and my mate and all the others. I'm coming."

"Your mate is here? I always dreamed of a mate, but the Accords..."

Those were coming to an end. If I had to tear them into a million pieces myself.

———

I JOLTED AWAKE, nearly elbowing Preston in the nose when I did. He managed to catch my elbow and save himself the pain just in the nick of time.

"Sorry." I tried to clear my head while holding onto the information. "Quick. Write this down."

He grabbed a notebook and took down what I told him. Getting it out, I collapsed on top of him like my body was too heavy to keep upright. "Do you think we can work with that?"

"Yep. For sure." He ran his hands through my hair. "Breathe for me."

"I have to try for the others now."

He didn't say anything for a few moments. "I don't mind you getting more sleep. In fact, I hope that you can. But you have to take a second. You aren't going to be a machine about this. You'll never fall back asleep again. You can't force it. Take a little time. Then try again. We'll get there. I promise."

I lifted my head. "I love how you say we."

"There's nothing you go through I wouldn't gladly change places to bear for you."

I stared at his lovely face. There was only the smallest

amount of light in the room. He must have been reading one of Anton's books. He'd set it aside. "Preston, when I first met you, I thought you might be mean. You were standoffish. Jarret was nicer. You intimidated me a little bit; I was kind of out of it, and you've turned out to be this incredibly kind, big-hearted man. You're just the most amazing person I could imagine."

He continued to run his hands through my hair. "You scared the shit out of me. The second Gus carried you up to the house I freaked out. Beautiful girl I was going to be responsible for? Werewolf girl? And then you shifted." He paused, his gaze far away, almost like he could see those moments again. "And I caught a whiff of you, and I knew for sure what I'd been pretty positive about anyway—you were mine. Mine, baby. I'm sorry that they could take control of me like that. I'm so sorry. I'd have died first if I'd had any way to know what was coming."

I pressed my head down on his chest to hear his heartbeat. "No. I need you. You came back. Promise me you'll always come back, and it'll be enough."

His arms came around me. "I promise."

We stayed like that for a while. He was right. I hadn't been able to just close my eyes and immediately go right back to bed, to find Rainer and Anton. It hadn't worked like that. The hours ticked by. Eventually, my eyes closed.

WE RECONVENED at the table early in the morning to mark the locations I had confirmed. I hadn't reached Rainer and Anton, but others who were near them. Miranda didn't have an answer as to why that would be, and I was making guesses in my own head. Maybe I'd sent my Omega wolf signal in their direction and been intercepted by the other wolves who were with them. Maybe the fact that I didn't have the marks made it impossible to do this at all. Frustration was making me churlish and snappy. I didn't like either of those qualities about myself.

In any case, we were pretty sure we had a solid idea where many were. Cars pulled up and came to screeching stops in the driveway. I looked at Miranda. "You're sure you want to send your pack out on this with us?"

She nodded. "Darling, they know we're here now. They will come for us. I believe in fate. Your mate told me his whole theory about how we pick each other in mating, and I disagree whole-heartedly with him. There is such a thing as fated mates. For werewolves there is meant to be. And that tells me that things happen for a reason. You came to me for a reason." She hugged me, which jarred me, and I somehow had to get used to people doing that again. "I'm meant to help you. Maybe my sister sent you my way. She'd want me to help the only living Omega. In fact, she'd kick my butt from here to Alaska if I didn't. We'll go get the wolves from these corporate types who have them."

This close to her, I could say what had niggled at my mind from the beginning. "Does this feel corporate to you? They can't be making any money on this. And hunters kill us, they don't experiment in ways that make sense to me, in ways that might elicit money for them."

She went very still. "What do you think? That man, Brennan, lied?"

"Or he was lied to." I let go of her. "I'm not sure. Frankly, I just need to figure this out so I can know whose ass I have to destroy once we get all our werewolves back."

She took my cheeks in her hands. "I've never known an

Omega with revenge in her heart before. Be careful. You guys are usually pretty good at turning the other cheek."

Not me. But maybe that was why I was here and none of the rest of them were. I didn't have the luxury of feeling like some kind of spiritual pack-driven healer. I was here, in survival mode, until things cooled down and I could afford to be otherwise. Whoever was doing this had fucking taken what belonged to me. I'd save everyone as soon as I got them back. But I would make someone pay for this, and my wolf would enjoy licking up their blood in the process.

PRESTON FELL ASLEEP, his head leaning against the passenger window of the RV as we drove out toward Atlanta.

My brother Isaac changed lanes like he'd driven one of these things a million times and expertly knew how to handle it. I sat on a couch where I was supposed to be resting, but I doubted I'd get to rest any time soon.

I lifted my gaze to Preston. He'd been up all night, every night with me. This was going to catch up with him, fast.

Goosebumps broke out on my arms, and my stomach clenched. It was the same feeling I'd had when I made us go to Miranda's town. "Isaac, I need you to get off the road."

He looked at me in the rearview mirror. "What? Now? We've hardly been on the road an hour. You okay?"

"Now. Next exit. I need you to trust me. It's my nose or my ears, or something wolf, okay? It's an Omega thing. Isaac, so help me, I need you to pull off into the rest area. Now. I don't need to see it to know it's there. I just do."

He nodded, and Preston opened his eyes. "Something wrong?"

"The Omega needs me to pull over."

Preston glared at him. "Then I'm going to suggest you fucking do as she says."

"You're all going to have to cut me a break. I woke up from a fog to discover my sister is now to be treated like every word she says is gospel. I once sat for three hours and drank pretend tea with her. There's a little adjusting going on, particularly that you even exist, and your three brothers in her life. But, yes, I'm pulling the fuck over."

Rolling his eyes, Preston answered him. "I bet it was the best tasting pretend tea ever."

Isaac laughed, throwing his head back. "Yes. Okay. It totally was. Agustin wakes up from hell, and he at least gets a mate out of the whole thing."

Preston patted him on the shoulder as we came to a stop. "When the Accords are officially gone, everyone will start to find their mates again. Maybe try not to be such a grumpy guy when you meet her. It might be a little off putting."

I got to my feet. "Hit the button. Open the door. Lower the stairs. Come on. Now."

They could be as amusing as they wanted to be. It hadn't altered a thing about my need to get into that rest stop right this second. Isaac did it, but I didn't wait for the stairs, jumping down as fast as I could.

"Hey," Preston called after me. "Wait on me. Nowhere without me, Mac."

"Who calls her Mac?" Isaac asked as he must have, based on the sound of his voice, been trailing after Preston.

I skidded to a stop in front of the building that held the bathrooms, recognizing immediately why I had been brought here. There were five werewolves. They stood in the corner, one of them holding a bag of ice they must have just bought from the machine inside. They all turned to look at me at once, but I only had eyes for one of them.

Rainer.

There was a group heading to Boston where I'd thought he'd be. Yet here he was. He wasn't alone. There were four others with him. Including his father Cristian. They were all right there. Five male werewolves. They growled at the same time as Preston and my brother, which made the whole rest stop explode with the sounds of human voices resembling wolves. I shook my head. We were all alone for the moment. Maybe Miranda was right about this fate thing.

"Second on the left is Rainer, my oldest brother," Preston told Isaac.

That was the last thing any of us said. These guys hadn't known I would be here anymore than I had known they would be. Yet, there we were. I might not have been their target, but it didn't mean they hadn't been told to kill me if they saw me. There was probably a universal kill order for me.

My hands burned, and this time it was with the right-eous need to take back what was mine, to make him stop smelling like the metallic stink that had overtaken him. I would fix them all, but right then, I only had eyes for Rainer.

I shifted.

If humans showed up in this rest area, they were going to be in for a deep shock. I couldn't bring myself to give a shit.

Rainer shifted, charging at me, but Preston intercepted him, knocking him down. They wrestled, but Preston came out on top. Two of the other wolves launched at Preston. While Rainer was down, I jumped on him. I'd talk to Pres later. I could have handled Rainer. It didn't matter. My power pushed out at Rainer.

He growled at me before he tore into my neck. I cried out but didn't let go. Leave it to Rainer to go for the jugular. My brother and Preston must have brought down everyone else. That was good. If I didn't bleed to death, I'd help them all next.

SIX

Good news, I didn't bleed out. I shifted into my human form and then back again, a gut-wrenching pain telling me this was almost too much. But if I didn't do it, I'd never make it through this. My brother threw himself on Rainer, keeping him pinned. Preston growled. I was back in my wolf form. Physically healed. I leaped on my oldest mate again. I was getting him back. I was getting them all back, damn it.

Hours later, healed and cleansed of the metallic scent, they slept off the remaining pain from their mind imprisonment. All of them were unconscious and prone on the two couches and blankets on the floor.

My brother held some of the ice the wolves had been buying from the ice machine inside against his cheek. He winced and laughed. "You really are an Omega."

I lifted my head from where I'd laid it in Preston's lap. "The fact that I saved your ass escaped you?"

He shook his head. "I don't remember it. I believed you. But seeing it. First of all, that was a wolf fight. I can't remember having those before, either. And now I've actually witnessed you do your thing. You're kind of a miracle."

Preston kissed my temple. "Nothing kind of about it. She's a fucking miracle."

"Yeah." Isaac got to his feet. "Okay. Driving to Atlanta, unless someone is stopping me."

We weren't getting there tonight. I was too tired to do this. "I don't think I can help anyone else until tomorrow."

My brother nodded. "Fair enough. What were they going to do with the ice? I'm glad they did. I managed to bang the fuck out of myself dragging them in here, but seriously? Why were they buying ice?"

Preston shook his head. "I doubt they'll remember. Let's decide it's fortuitous. Do you think I could get you to lie on the bed for a while, Mac?"

I wouldn't argue. "Sure. If anyone needs me, I'll be in there. I can even drive if you want. I'm wide-awake."

"Shouldn't that have knocked her out? It was a ton of power." He talked to Preston like I wasn't there.

"Totally annoying how you're doing that," I snapped at Isaac. "It used to knock me out."

I threw a look at Rainer who breathed easily on the couch before I let Preston settle me on the bed. At some point, Isaac put the RV back in motion. Preston left to go keep him company, in case he needed help. I didn't sleep. Instead, I sort of floated. I'd meant what I'd said to Miranda. This didn't feel corporate. It was almost personal.

And I might have been tired and half out of my mind, but I wasn't wrong. That much I knew. The question was why.

THE SOUNDS of voices drifted into the room where I lay —exactly where Preston had left me. Three of them were new, but Rainer and Cristian's weren't. I should get up and go out to them, but I'd officially hit my point of no return. I couldn't help anyone else, because I was done. I didn't have anything left to give.

Tears flooded my eyes. Maybe Miranda was right. Maybe I was dying, and I just hadn't realized that I only had one fight left to give. I'd expended it. Jarret and Anton were going to forever be lost, because I was going to float away to nothingness. A failed Omega who really accomplished nothing.

The door opened and closed. Rainer's scent filled the room. He was awake. I lifted my head as the bed dipped from his weight.

"Hey," I said as his arm came around me. Rainer fitted himself against my side. "You're okay."

His eyes widened, meeting my gaze. "I am, thanks to you, MacKenzie. But you're not. Preston has filled me in. I sort of understand. Enough for tonight, anyway." He ran his hand under my shirt, touching me, skin-to-skin. Heat traveled through me. This was Rainer. He was *here*.

"I'm not doing well. I keep trying to pull it together. I keep saying that I'll get through it, but tonight, I don't think I can. Tonight, I'm so sorry, but I think I'm just done. I don't have one more ounce of strength left, and I don't think it's coming back. I think..."

Rainer kissed my nose. "You're exhausted. I can feel it in my pores. It's burning my tongue. And how could you not be? You sleep half an hour at night, assaulted by other people's needs even in that time, and then you are asked to continue to perform day after day as though you've had the rejuvenation you need."

Well, he'd summed that up pretty well. "Yes. Plus, I have this empty inside of me. It whips and beats, and wants to hurt the people around me. Preston stilled it a little bit, but it's still there. I'm sorry. That must sound senseless."

"I don't have to understand it to know that it's real to you." He rubbed my back, the moves gentle. "I need to look and see that my mark is gone. Okay? I know that Preston told me, but I need to see for myself."

I nodded. He was more than welcome to take a gander at the empty space where his mark should have been. With his free hand, he tugged on my shirt just enough to look down. He visibly swallowed and let it go.

"I did it. I didn't mean to, but I guess it's something I did to myself, because I know that it's my fault this all happened. Some sort of punishment I self-imposed. I..."

He leaned on his elbow. "Stop blaming yourself. Whatever the reasons this happened, it's not on you. We're going to get through this, and to start, I'm going to give you back my mark."

I sighed. "I'd love to have it back, and there's nothing I'd want more than to make love to you, Rainer. But I don't have the energy to even think about sex. I can't..."

"I didn't say anything about that. We'll get to that after you're better. I'm not thinking about sex. I'm thinking there is a reason mates wear each other's mark. I can feel you on my skin, you're like a protection against the world for me. I always know you're there. You shouldn't be doing your Omega duties without us constantly with you. I'm going to mark you, and even though it's all been related to sex up until now, that's not a necessity. Lift your arms."

I managed to do as he asked, and he pulled my shirt over my head. Rainer dropped his head, taking a deep breath against my skin where his mark should have been. Warmth moved through me, and I wished I wasn't so wiped. A second later, he bit down. I yelped. I hadn't expected it, but the pain soon stopped, replaced by a shudder of pleasure. He lapped at the bite with his tongue.

I giggled. It was a strange response, but the empty inside of me shrank, and in its place, a sort of elation took root. Oh, it wasn't gone. No, the empty bounced and dove around, but it had less space to occupy.

He lifted his head, licking his lips. "What's funny?"

"Nothing really. Second time you've gone for my neck tonight."

Rainer furrowed his brow. "I'm so sorry if I hurt you. I don't remember anything. Literally nothing. We were home in Louisiana, and now we're here. It's a big old blank spot. I hurt you?"

I touched the side of his face. "I shifted. It's okay. It's not you anymore than Preston was the guy saying horrible things to me when he showed up. I'm just glad I found you. They had you out doing things for them. I don't know what, and who knows when I'd have stumbled upon you again." I swallowed. "Rainer, I don't want to die until I can fix Anton and Jarret. I don't want to go away knowing that they are still under the control of those terrible people."

He shook his head very slowly. "You're not dying. I won't allow it. No." He kissed me gently. "Let's get the rest of your clothes off. I want to be skin-to-skin with you. I need it, and so do you."

I managed to pull my pants off, and he did the same, fully undressing. I pressed my head against his chest to listen to his heartbeat. It was strong, steady. He was here. He stroked my back again as he held me close.

A light knock sounded before Preston poked his head in

the door. I drifted but could make out sounds as he came close to the bed, eventually tugging his own shirt off.

"What happens when you sleep?" Rainer kissed along my face, the end of my nose, both my cheekbones. "Preston explained, but I want you to tell me, okay?"

I lifted my head to stare at him. I hadn't known it was possible to have my gaze so tired, I couldn't even focus anymore. "They come to me. Ask me to help them. I can't. That causes me pain, and I wake up. The whole thing seems to take about thirty-two minutes every time. Let's say half an hour for the sake of rounding. But it's almost always exactly thirty-two minutes."

"Okay, the time is less important to me, except that it tells me just how exhausted you really are. You end up in pain, because you can't help. Preston said you were in a lot of pain when he first got here, but some of that has waned since he marked you again and you came back together."

I looked over my shoulder at Preston as he climbed in the bed behind me. He was also totally naked. Under other circumstances, this would be a dream come true.

"That's right. The aching, absolute mind-consuming awfulness had waned somewhat since Preston came back."

Rainer nodded. "So let's assume that you didn't have this dream problem when we were all together, because somehow having us with you let you block whatever the connection is that happens between you and needy wolves during sleep. You used it to hopefully locate Jarret and Anton. That's great. But now it's time to try to keep it away. Omegas always have strong mates. There are reasons for this that go beyond keeping sick wolves from breaking down doors at night. I'm here now. We're going to cuddle with you just like this. Skin-to-skin. They won't get through to you tonight. That is what I'm thinking is going to happen.

But if they do, rather than just rejecting helping them, ask them to come to Louisiana. If they can't, take down their location and tell us. We'll send someone to get them. Maybe then there won't be the pain, and you can just move on and stay asleep. There has to be a way to manage this. Omegas don't die from this."

I hoped that he was right. A tear fluttered down my cheek, and he smoothed it away with his thumb. I smiled at Rainer and drew Preston's arms around my stomach so he was close, too. "Or I might just be a very bad Omega. That is pretty much what Pres said to me when he was under mind control."

Preston sucked in a long breath. "You know I don't think that. And, hey, out of the two of us in here, Rainer is the one who went for your jugular."

Rainer winced. "We're the worst mates ever, Preston. But we're going to do better. I just had to promise your very cantankerous brother, Isaac, we would do better, because he was going to block the door."

I liked that word for him. I loved that I had two of my mates with me, and that I was toasty warm in between them. I didn't know what was happening on the other side of the door, and I was fine with not currently knowing.

Rainer said I wasn't going to die, and that maybe I could sleep. I had two marks on my body again. Those were beautiful things to think about.

"Thank you, Pres." Rainer's voice sounded rough, lower than usual. "For getting back to her faster. For keeping her alive. Thank you, brother."

"Thank you for being in that fucking rest stop, even if you don't know why you were."

I smiled. Their scents drifted over me.

I WOKE myself up with my snoring. It was a strange sensation, and not one I could ever remember having happened before. Light streamed in through the RV window, and the vehicle was moving. Clearly, someone was driving us somewhere, I just had no idea where.

I rubbed at my eyes. Pressed between Rainer and Preston, I was still exactly as I'd been when I closed my eyes. Only I didn't remember doing that, and it had been nighttime.

"I'm sorry. I was snoring."

Rainer turned his head to look at me, and Preston shifted, kissing my shoulder. "No, you weren't. Totally weren't. And you don't have to be up yet. Go back to sleep."

"Did I... did I sleep?"

My oldest mate grinned at me. "Yes, and you can some more. We've got plenty of time. Close those eyes again."

I wasn't sure that I could. My head was foggy, but there was light streaming in, and I wasn't achy in a way that made me want to burrow into the ground and never get out. "How long did I sleep?"

I loved Rainer's grin when he answered. "Twelve fucking hours."

"Really?" I sat up straight, which made both of them do it, too. "I didn't see anyone. Not any other wolves. I just slept."

Rainer nodded at Preston. "Two of us. She needs two of us in the bed. She's had that since night one. Even if we weren't there in the bed, we were all in that house. We're like the guardians of her energy."

Preston leaned against the headboard. "I'm going to go see what is happening out there. Get your brother to stop somewhere again. We've made about three long stops to charge this thing, and whatever else he was doing. Buy some junk food."

Rainer shook his head. "After we get to Atlanta and go back home, no more junk food."

Preston saluted him and winked at me. "This is really just me getting lost and giving you two some privacy. Everyone stayed quiet last night—mostly because your brother is scary. But I'm going to do better than that for you. Yes, I am the greatest mate of all time."

Rainer threw a pillow at him. I leaned back to gaze at Rainer as Pres left. He was so fucking handsome, and I hadn't imagined it. He was here. "Rainer, I love you."

He brought me to him so that we were face-to-face. "That's good, because I love you, too."

"I think you saved me."

He smirked. "Well, you saved me, so the least I could do was return the favor."

The RV slowed down as though someone was pulling off the road. I tilted my head to the side.

"So just to be sure I understand, Preston just got my brother or whoever is driving to pull over so everyone can get... so we can..."

Rainer cleared his throat. "Have sex. Yep."

My cheeks felt very heated. "I'm probably all red."

He ran his finger down my face. "What you look like is that you are bright-eyed as opposed to last night. Huge difference. I never want to see you like that again." He kissed my lips, and I smiled against his mouth. "I don't expect one night to fix it. You might need to sleep this much over and over, until you build back some strength. Whatever you need. Okay?"

Rainer was so ridiculously sweet. "You just came back

to me. Are you okay? You're the one I care about here." I lifted my hand. They weren't burning, but damn, I knew I couldn't count on that as really telling me anything. The whole problem with Anton illustrated that.

He kissed me again. "Sweetheart, I woke up just fine. Whatever happened, I don't remember, and I don't give a shit about it. The only thing that concerns me is that being away from you caused you so much pain. You needed me, and I wasn't here. I'm fine."

I pressed our lips together harder. Okay. If he wasn't suffering, then I needed him. Right then and there. All other thoughts fled from my mind. He wrapped me up against him before rolling us both over and covering me with his body. I loved the heavy feel of him on top of me. I craved this.

He scraped his fingers over the mark he'd given me the night before. I shuddered. "I'm so happy to have it back."

Rainer tilted his head. "When it wasn't there, I wanted to destroy the world. That is my spot, my sign that I belong to you. So the whole fucking world knows."

Well... I wasn't entirely sure that humans would know, but I didn't really care right then. We were both already naked, and he was mine. I could touch him everywhere. I ran my fingers over his back, digging my fingernails in slightly just to really confirm that I hadn't made him up. I wasn't delusional. He was there with me.

Rainer must have liked the slight bite of pain because he moaned, the most delicious sound. A second later, I was flipped over. I blinked. Okay. I was on my stomach, and he was right behind me. This was new.

He kissed both my shoulder blades before he licked down the center of my back. My nipples hardened, rubbing against the sheets on the bed. They ached. Now it was my turn to moan. Rainer squeezed my rear.

"Have I ever told you how much I love your ass?" Yes, he had mentioned that on more than one occasion, and he stared at it all the time. I loved it. He leaned over to whisper in my ear. "I fucking love your ass. Scoot up. Against the headboard. Hold onto it."

This was a whole new Rainer. I practically vibrated with anticipation. What was he going to do here? Rainer scooted up behind me. He pressed himself against me, and his hardness was evident, even from behind.

"I'm so fucking ready for you. You make me feel like I'm fifteen years old with a constant erection."

I smiled at that description. "I could turn around and..."

"No," he interrupted. "Stay right where you are." He bit down on my shoulder, a gentle nip. I doubted it would even leave a mark. "You taste like cherries." He sucked in a breath. "And somehow I'm even harder right now. How am I fucking harder?"

I wanted to touch him. "Rainer..."

"Not yet." He palmed my ass again. "I want you to know that you're mine. I want you to feel it. I want you to know that I'll take care of you."

I scrunched up my face. "I do know those things."

"I need to show you again."

He wasn't making a lot of sense, and that was okay. Right then, he didn't need to. I could smell his desire, like a warm aroma coming around me. Coupled with Rainer's usual woodsy scent, I was all but lost in a mess of feelings myself. He wanted me to feel his love for me, that he'd do anything for me. If his telling me that was a little rambling, I didn't care. I just wanted the words, and even more, I wanted him to feel that way.

Rainer sucked in a long, audible breath. "The time away is a blank slate for me, like it didn't happen, but my body knows it did. It feels like an eternity since I've been inside of you."

He squeezed my nipples, and I cried out. From behind, he massaged my breasts, his hips moving gently as he pressed his cock against my rear and then away from it again. Over and over. "You're mine."

I leaned back against him. Rainer caused jolts of pleasure to move through me, but he wasn't giving me what I needed. It was like he tortured both of us. "I am. I promise, I'm yours."

He dropped one of his hands and slipped his finger over me, moving it slightly until he could press on my clit. I cried out. Rainer kissed my neck, not saying a word as he built the pressure inside of me until I squirmed against him, pushing my ass against his cock as he continued to move against me. He moaned in my ear.

It was the best sound ever. I leaned my head back, able to see his eyes. They were slits. "So fucking wet."

"Rainer. Please. I want to come, but not on your fingers. I want to come with you inside of me." I needed to feel filled by him. This wasn't going to be enough.

He rubbed his forehead against my shoulder and let go of me. With his strong hands, he adjusted my position a little but didn't turn me around. Instead, he pressed inside of me from behind, filling my pussy in one hard stroke. I cried out. From this position, he really had leverage to fill me. It was a dominant, passionate move, and I loved every second of it.

The only thing I couldn't do was kiss him. I did miss his lips. But then, I couldn't think at all. He'd been still since he moved inside of me. Not now. He moved slowly, not faster than he had been when he'd been pressing against me earlier. It was the sweetest torture.

"Love you," he whispered in my ear, and experience told me he was about to be as lost to this as I was. It was in the tone of his voice, the way that I could hear the ache in the words he spoke.

"Yes." I sighed. "I love you, too."

He picked up his pace, and I had to hold onto the headboard for dear life. In and out of me he thrust and pressed back in. Each pass was like he'd pulled all the way out and come right back.

"More. Please." It was all I could say. "Yes, please."

Now it was my turn to be nonsensical. Fuck. I loved this man. I dropped one of my hands from the headboard to hold him. I loved the way we looked together as pleasure rode me, as it threatened to take me over the top into orgasm. This was my Rainer. He'd left, but he was back.

I was close. "Soon," I managed to say, because I wanted him to hear it.

"I know," he whispered in my ear. "I can always read your body. Come for me, beautiful. I'll follow you. I promise. From now on."

Maybe those were the words I needed to hear. He grabbed me and pulled me against him, his cock stroking right along my clit when he pulled out just before he pressed back in. I cried out, arching against him, which must have been what he needed, too. We both hit the climax together. He panted against me, and I sobbed. I didn't try to stop the tears. This was the release I desperately needed.

I leaned against him. Yes, Rainer was with me. I could believe it now. As long as he kept reminding me.

SEVEN

"MacKenzie." Cristian rose when I came out of the bedroom. Rainer had exited ahead of me, and I'd heard the sounds of people coming back in as I'd dressed. I ached everywhere. Less pain than before Preston came, and certainly my head was clearer with Rainer's return. But I wasn't fixed. I didn't know if this was going to get any better with Jarret and Anton, or if this was going to be my new normal. I yawned. I'd slept twelve hours, and now it felt like I needed a nap.

I'd taken being a high-energy person for granted, that was for sure.

My father-in-law embraced me in a tight hug. "Thank you. Thank you for saving my boys."

I hugged him back. "I'm so glad I could get you back. I won't stop until I have all of you, or I just... die trying."

"There's not going to be any dying," Preston shouted from the passenger seat of the RV. That seemed to be his spot. My brother drove, and Preston sat up there with him.

Isaac shook his head. "I can't think of anything I hate more than exiting a vehicle so my sister can have sex in it."

I threw something at him, and he ducked. Preston rolled his eyes but otherwise ignored him, and Rainer shot my oldest brother daggers from his gaze. I wouldn't want to be on the other end of a look from Rainer like that one. Cristian took a seat next to Rainer, and I joined him on the other side. My oldest mate put his arm around me, and Isaac pulled us out into traffic.

His father elbowed Rainer. "I've never been so grateful your mother didn't have brothers."

I rubbed my eyes. "We're going to get everyone back. Your wife, my mother. Everyone." Somehow, I would be strong enough. Internally, I snorted. I wasn't nearly strong enough. Not anywhere close to it. But, somehow, I'd have to be.

One of the new wolves in the RV with us who had been with Rainer at the rest stop was named Dylan Wisdom. He stared at my tablet. "It's been years, and I have no idea where I've been, or what I've done. Not that I was doing anything particularly important before I vanished. Weird to feel like I can shift, like I have a wolf inside of me. What are our plans when we get to where we're going and find the particular building where they're holding more people like us?"

Preston winced as the man spoke. "I'm sorry you lost so much time. We're going to storm through the door and kill every human in there. Take back our people. If anyone has trouble with that, you're welcome to stay in the RV."

Dylan's gaze turned wolf. "Yes, they hurt us, they die. It's that simple."

Rainer tugged on the end of my hair. "You okay?"

I turned to look at him. "I'm fine."

The sad truth was, I really was. I guessed I'd really crossed into the zone where anyone who got in our way deserved to be gotten rid of. They had my mates. They were hurting people, and anyone who worked there, who participated in the pain, well, yes, I was fine with that. We were sentient beings, we looked like them, talked like them, and we damn well felt like them. They treated us like lab rats? Yes, they could see what kinds of monsters we really were.

My mouth watered, and I wanted to shift. Rainer squeezed my leg, and I smiled at him. My eyes had gone wolf. It had been a little while since that happened spontaneously. He leaned over to rub his forehead against my cheek. I relished in the touch. Preston turned around from where he sat and winked at me. I needed these moments, these small displays of affection.

"Are you sure you're an Omega?" Dylan lifted his eyebrows. "Ours was just an old woman who never said a mean word about anyone. I hardly knew her."

I tilted my head. "Well, if you hardly knew her, then I'm not sure how you can tell what she thought and didn't think. But, fine, if that is the case, if all the Omegas were sweet healers who were happy to take pack problems on their own and basically live a life of waiting for the next abuse with no retribution... well, then I guess you're right. I guess I am a terrible Omega."

Preston closed his eyes. "I'm bored with this. She's the best there ever was, and anyone who says anything differently, I'll tear out their fucking throat, and Rainer won't let you fix them."

I smiled. Maybe I wasn't the only one wanting to bathe in the blood of enemies right then. If I was wearing fur to do it, then even better.

IT WASN'T hard to find where we were going in Atlanta. My brother used the parameters I'd given him to search the Internet on a phone he'd palmed from someone at a rest stop. We ended up in the Fulton Industrial District in no time.

Eventually, we pulled over, and I just tried to breathe. We'd have to find the specific spot, and I was sure it was going to be that stench, that metallic, awful, mind-numbing disgustingness that would lead me right to them. Could I locate it in the middle of a city with no idea where to look? Probably not. Could I locate it within a small area? Yes, I could. I fucking could.

We walked. There was a large empty lot with nothing in it, and I really didn't believe that they inhabited an abandoned building. No, they were going to need to take food deliveries. Clothing. Preston hadn't been in any of his own stuff when he'd come back to me. Wherever he was, someone had dressed him. They had to be able to move stuff in and out. I doubted that they were hiding all their deliveries in the middle of the night. No, in this day and age of satellites, the trick had to be to hide in plain sight. The same way werewolves had done it before we stopped shifting altogether.

They were going to be in a nondescript building with legitimate businesses right next door. I chewed on my lips as we approached a group of them. Warehouses that were being used for holding imports and... I stared at the building in the center. Commercial. Windows we couldn't see inside. I breathed.

My nose was good... for picking up distress and other emotions. I looked at Preston. His was better. "Getting anything metallic from there?" I nodded toward the one I couldn't take my eyes off of. My hands burned but that could just have meant that one of the guys I was with was having an issue. The longer I did this, the better I was getting at controlling it. I didn't have to react to every need that came my way immediately. That was a change from what it had been just days earlier. Of course, if a Loup showed up, that might be different. And I was sure when I ran into captured wolves, I'd need to fix them right away, too.

Preston sniffed the air. "I am, actually." He pointed to his mouth. "Like I can taste it on my tongue."

That's what I thought. "They're in there. Or someone is that we need to get to."

Rainer stepped next to me. "Okay. We're going in."

I nodded. "This isn't where you try to get me to stay outside, right? Because I think I can tell you how that discussion will go."

He smirked at me. "Even if I used my most severe Alpha tone?"

"Do you have a severe Alpha tone?" I hadn't heard one yet. But that was fine. "In that event, I'm sure I'll want to look at the ground and not make eye contact with you. Having said that, I'm still going in."

He tugged on the end of my hair. "I know you are. But remember the cage with Agustin? We're not repeating that problem. So you'll go in behind me, and you'll stay back if I indicate that. In your human form, or your wolf form. That is a line I'm drawing, not as some kind of Alpha thing, but because I love you, and you've been through hell."

I nodded. "Okay. That's fine. I'll stay back. But if I have to fight, I'm going to, and you know I can do that."

He palmed my cheek. "I sure do. Apparently, you took me on just fine. It isn't that I don't believe in you. I do. But I need to keep you as safe as I can, given the circumstances."

"All right, I agree. I'll stay behind you. I'll do my best to not make this any harder on any of us. As best I can."

He smiled at me. "Love you, MacKenzie Harper. Let's get this done."

Rainer shifted. He really was a beautiful wolf. Big, scary, and able to take on anything. I was just glad this time he wasn't going to come after me. I stared down at him. "If they take you back, I'm going to be really pissed. But I'm going to come get you. No matter how many times that takes."

He shook his head and huffed at me before he turned and ran into the building. The others chased after him, except for Preston who waited by the door. The sound of gunfire erupted, and I rushed forward, but he grabbed me.

"Not yet. It's not us being hurt." He smiled at me. "I can scent the humans pissing themselves. Can't you?"

I took a deep breath. "I can." I smiled at him. "We're so sick in the head that we like this so much, aren't we?"

"We're wolves." Preston licked my neck, and I shuddered. "And we bathe in the blood of those who hurt our packs. So shift, and let's get to it. By the way, every time you look, you're going to find me right next to you. Let's go get our people."

I called the shift onto myself. It was weird doing this out in public, but with everything happening, I guessed whether or not we got spotted ranked lowest on the list of things to worry about. I smiled. Let the world get a good look.

I rushed forward, following my nose. There was blood in the main hallway and at the reception desk. Maybe later I'd feel badly, but not so far. Rainer was ahead, and I moved toward his scent until I veered toward another one. We hadn't cleared the direction yet and somewhere else people—humans—screamed. I counted on those I was with to deal with them. I'd caught a whiff of who I needed to get to.

The stench of sick wolf met my nose. They needed me. Preston growled at me, pushing in front of me to go through the door. This place had been designed with wolves in mind. The doors swung open with just a push. I wasn't focused on human things like money right then, but in the back of my head, I couldn't help but wonder how any of this worked. I would have to figure it out later.

As it was, I found a room full of shifters, shaking and rocking in chairs. No one smelled right, so I forced my eyes up to see if I could identify who I looked at. Did I know any of them? Like he was a magnet, I locked onto Jarret. I whined, and Preston followed my gaze. There he was. Part of my heart. There were five others in this room. Gus was here. And my mother. Two others I didn't know. I cared about all of them, but I wanted Jarret.

Could we get him out of here while we were wolves, and he was shaking like that as a human? Why was he doing that? I growled, not out of anger but fear. No part of me liked what I was seeing here, not my wolf, not my human. I shifted into my human form. They needed immediate help, and if I wasn't wrong, then I was pretty sure they couldn't currently shift either. These were the shifters who weren't making it. What had been done to them in the meantime? What steps had been taken?

Jarret didn't recognize me when I approached him.

"Here." Preston's voice caught my attention, but I couldn't take my eyes off Jarret. He was so hurt. "Wrap up in this. It's a lab coat. Smells clean."

I nodded my thanks while Preston basically dressed me, affixing the front with a belt. I would otherwise have been naked. I didn't care, but he was right to want us to be covered. Danger could still come through the door.

Preston touched his brother's shoulder. "She's got you, Brother."

He walked away from me toward Gus. A thought dawned on me, and I turned toward him. "Pres, that's my mom next to him."

He raised his eyebrows. "She's going to be fine, too. I'll keep her safe while you do your thing here. In the meantime, I fully expect Rainer and the others any second. You've been too long out of his vision."

I turned my attention fully back to Jarret. Leaning over, I kissed his cheek. "If you can hear me, it's going to get better."

I pulled him into my arms and let my power loose. It came out like a burn, like a scorch. I shook with him, and although it had never happened before, for a second, I could see what he saw. Dancing stars, twisting colors. Screeching noises. Wolves howling. Nothing was clear. Nothing was real. A loud high-pitched noise I couldn't get out of my ears. Still, I hung on, and it dimmed. Was that what it was like for everyone when they were taken? And then what? Did the humans replace the noise with their own command?

I guessed, but really, I didn't have a clue. I was sure of one thing. I wasn't in the presence of hunters here. This was something else. My attention fled entirely back to Jarret. I hung on. I was going to bring him—all of them—back to themselves.

Preston's hand touched my back. They didn't usually make contact with me when I healed, but I appreciated feeling it right then. He held onto me, kept me here, kept me grounded. Today wasn't the day that I was going to fall apart.

I SAT ON THE FLOOR, still in the lab coat, and watched as the others carried the newly healed wolves out. The building was filled with dead humans. No police had been called. Preston stood next to where I sat, watching over things.

"You okay, Mac?" He winked at me. "You did that fast. Like, I think that was a record. You're really starting to get a knack for it."

I shook my head. "I don't feel done."

Rainer strode over and knelt down. Everyone had managed to grab clothes off the humans. We wouldn't draw attention to ourselves by being naked outside. Other reasons, maybe we would. I still couldn't bring myself to care.

"Are you feeling like you need to fix us because some of us got injuries?"

I did want to do that, but no. I got to my feet. "Bear with me for a little bit. Is it safe to walk around?"

Rainer nodded. "Sure. Great job keeping her safe. Take the others outside. I want to sleep in motel rooms tonight, but put Jarret in the main bedroom in the RV so he's with us. Gus with Cristian. And her mom on the big couch. Yes, they're benefiting from nepotism. I don't care."

Preston patted Rainer's arm. "I'll make sure everyone is good. Even the two we don't know. Especially since everyone here is talking about joining our so-called pack, and you are about to have to lead all of them."

Rainer visibly paled. "What?"

"Yep."

I walked past them. Rainer said it was safe. He'd catch up.

I sniffed the air. I'd had this happen to me before. The first time I'd made Rainer and Jarret take me to find the Loups who got away. It was like I had just followed the feeling. I was doing it again. Rainer rushed up, grabbing my hand.

"So, this is a you-are-in-a-hurry thing."

I was bone deep tired. "I have to keep going until I'm done. Period. The longer I wait, the more I'm going to need to crash. That won't make this easier. Someone is still here. Maybe more than one person."

"Got it." He squeezed my fingers. "You never cease to amaze me."

"I'm basically a walking battery waiting to make everyone feel better. I'm like the pack's power button. And right now, I'm the only one." I sighed. "Sorry, woe is me."

He shook his head. "No one feels that way about you except you. The rest of us are in awe. Period. When we get home, I'm going to just cook and cook for you. Good food in your stomach goes a long way. You've lost a lot of weight. You're gorgeous, but I need to feed you. It's like a primal need."

I abruptly stopped. I pointed at the wall. "There."

He stared at me, tilting his head. "Nothing is there."

"Sure there is. We just can't see it. But I can sense it." I strode to the wall. "Something is back there."

He leaned back. "Really? They have a hidden door? Like out of a movie. All right. What do we do?"

I closed my eyes and reached out. Somewhere there would be something to press. I breathed. It was hard to scent anything other than Rainer. When my mates were close, they were pretty all consuming. Particularly when I was tired, I just wanted to cuddle. But I had a job to do, and damn it, I was going to do it.

There was a difference in how the wall felt in one place and in another. I pressed where it felt thinner and something clicked. A door I'd never have been able to see opened.

"Shit." Rainer darted in front of me just as I opened my eyes. "I go first."

I waited a beat and followed him. There were five people in the room. They stood very still, on their feet, staring at the floor. Three men. Two women. Like before, I only had eyes for one of them.

Anton.

I forced myself to swallow. They'd both been here. Jarret and Anton. Rainer ran to Anton. "Bro? Can you hear me?"

He didn't respond. Unlike Jarret, who had been visibly shaking, Anton had no movement at all. It was everything I could do to convince myself he breathed. I stepped toward him. What was this room? It was all white. There were chairs, but no one sat on them. They all just stood.

Goosebumps broke out on my arms. We were being watched. Rainer must have sensed it, too. He looked up at the ceiling. "Smile at the audience."

I looked up at it. Who watched from there? I didn't run. Instead, I made sure I was in the center of the room. "I know you're not corporate. And I know you're not hunters. So who are you? I'm going to find out. However many you take... I will take back."

Rainer shook his head. "Fuck. Let's get out of here. Here, I'll take these three. You hold Anton's hand and that woman in the corner. They'll walk with us."

I did as he asked. If he objected to what was definitely my declaration of war, he didn't say so. What was he going to do? I couldn't take it back. I swallowed. We were well toward the front door before I spoke again.

"Rainer, did I make a huge mistake?"

"No. They were coming anyway, and they've already wanted you more than any of us. You just told them to fuck off. I kind of loved it."

Preston bounded out of the RV. "Holy shit."

I wasn't done, but I'd fix all of them on the RV. We had to get back to the swamp. I was a person who had to work on instinct. Mine were telling me to get home, and fast. We got on board. I needed Anton, but there were things to do. Details. Isaac sat with my mom, holding her in his lap. I smiled at the sight. "Call Miranda. Find out how it went with them."

"Already did. They've got everyone they could find."

I loved when things went according to plan. With way too many people in the RV, we headed toward Louisiana. I walked to Anton who sat, seeming to see nothing. My powers blared and around me everyone who was awake gasped. It was like my abilities had just shouted, and even those not hurt had heard them.

I wrapped my arms around Anton, and I held on tight.

EIGHT

I ran through a dark hallway, looking left and right. Where was everyone? What was happening? Why was I all alone? A tear slid down my cheek. I wiped it away.

"MacKenzie." Rainer's voice drifted over me. "Come back. Don't get lost in there."

I took a deep breath and rushed back into my body. I knelt in the RV, holding onto Anton. This was different than healing the others. Anton was in there, but it was like they had... it was like they had nudged him away in his own mind. I had to find him, and it wasn't easy. I chewed on my bottom lip.

I'd been trying for hours. I looked around. We must have stopped. The only people left on the RV were Preston, Rainer, Anton, Jarret, and myself. Everyone else had been moved off. "Are we home?"

Rainer spoke up. "No. Stopped at a motel. Everyone needed to sleep. I don't want you going back to the house and taking on every problem that the other rescued people will have. We stopped."

I supposed that made sense. "I didn't get him. Obviously." I stared at Anton. This was my third time delivering this news. I wanted to beat something bloody in frustration. "Why can't I find him? It's like I'm in his mind. That isn't how this works and yet, that is what is happening."

Preston kissed my cheek. "Mac, we don't know how any of this works. I don't know that any other Omega has ever had to deal with this."

That was probably true. I swallowed. "What if I can't fix him?"

"You can," Rainer interrupted, picking me off the floor. "I know you can. But you need a shower. Some food. Sleep. Even if it's another twelve hours. And then, frankly, you need Jarret to wake up and mark you again."

I smiled. "Well, it's really something when one of your mates wants you to have sex with another one."

Rainer rolled his eyes. "At no point did I say sex, but fine. Yes. Come on. Preston's going to take Anton in with us and come back for Jarret. We have connecting rooms. Everyone is comfortable. I've seen to it. Now, you, and then we get on with it. Tomorrow you can manage whatever faces us in Louisiana."

I knew he was right. Still, I had to ask him. "Don't you want to just get home? I feel like I need to be there, more than I need anything else in the world."

"That's the wolf. Yes, I feel it, too. We're craving pack lands. We come from the bayou, or at least werewolves lived there for more generations than I'd like to count. We started this mating there, we made it our home. I totally get it. But we're sleeping in this hotel because right now, I'm not convinced home is going to be restful."

Fair enough. "They took you guys from there. It's also not necessarily safe..."

"This time, it will be safe." A muscle ticked in his jaw. I could scent his tension. Rainer was on edge. Big time.

I touched the side of his face. "It wasn't your fault, you know. There wasn't a thing you could have done."

"Yeah... you aren't the only one who blames themselves for things. There were lots of things I could have done. Doesn't matter now. We can play the blame game later."

As we stepped outside, it started to rain. Rainer hurried his steps while he did his best to cover me with himself. I giggled. "I can walk. I'm not that bad off, thanks to you and Preston."

"I know. Maybe I like holding you." He winked at me.

That was the last thing I saw before I found myself back in that hallway looking for Anton. I spun around. What was happening? How had I gotten here? Was I healing him again?

Was I trying? Did I just not remember? "Anton?" I shouted.

Whatever was happening, he was somewhere around here. This was his prison, where those who had taken him from us had forced him to stay. But it was empty everywhere I looked. I steeled my back.

I refused to believe that he was empty, that he was gone.

"Anton." I forced myself to stop walking. I was going to stay right where I was. "Anton, it's MacKenzie. Can you hear me? Are you here?" I waited, but I heard nothing at all. "Anton, I'm here, and I need you to come to me."

A sound caught my attention. There were footsteps. In that second, Anton stood in front of me. He panted, staring at me with his mouth hanging open.

I took a tentative step toward him. "Anton, do you know me?"

He tilted his head, staring at me. I didn't expect him to

answer. We were in his head. Could he speak in here? I had no idea. But I'd never heard his voice. I wasn't looking for it now.

His whole face fell as he ran a hand through his hair. Whatever he was thinking, he didn't like it. I realized a second before he moved that he meant to run.

"No." I darted forward, and I grabbed his hand. "I'm with you. I need you."

He had so much pain in his eyes, that I couldn't stand it. I shook from the sheer agony he radiated back to me. He reached out with his free hand and placed it on top of my heart.

I swallowed. "You're worried that you hurt me, that it is something you did."

I pulled him up against me. "This is not on you. Not even a little bit. Anton, I am trying to heal you. But I can't. Not without your help. I need you to come back to me. Please. I am not okay without you guys, and I can't seem to fix you. I need you to tell me how."

He placed his head right in that spot where he always did. *I'm not sure you can. They've had me for so long, beautiful.*

I heard him. As though he'd spoken to me. I lifted my head and grabbed onto his cheeks so he'd look at me. "Yes. I can. You buried your pain. You made it so hard to get to that I couldn't even find it. I get it. How did you live with all of this your whole life, and everything that happened because of it? None of it was on you. Not one minute of it. They used you, Anton. And I am going to make it so they never can again, but I need you to feel it. I need you to bring it up closer to the surface so I can help you. I know that is hard. Unbelievably hard. But I need you to do this."

I let the tears I needed to shed fall down my cheeks. "Please. Try. For me. Please."

He wiped one of my tears away. *Okay. For you, beautiful. I'll try.*

I gasped, waking up in Rainer's arms. He stared down at me. "Are you okay? What the fuck just happened? It was like you just weren't there in your eyes." He growled at me, his wolf showing, and I reached up to stroke his cheek. I'd scared him, and I hadn't meant to. I hadn't even known that was going to happen.

"Let's get inside. I might be able to heal Anton now. I think... I think I convinced him to try?"

Preston stopped walking. "He didn't want to?"

"This is our youngest brother. He's guilt-ridden. I would be. He probably thought it better he stayed away, if he could think that clearly at all. He's probably lost in his own version of the pea soup existence we had going on."

I hoped that was true. If it was more like he just didn't have any confidence in my ability to do this, I was going to be heartbroken. Or if I'd left him to suffer for so long, he didn't want to try anymore. Sadness wafted through me.

A bang behind us made me jump in Rainer's arms. The door to the RV opened, and Jarret stumbled out. He looked around, his palm pressing against his forehead.

"Jarret." I struggled in Rainer's hold, and he put me down. The second my feet touched the ground, I rushed to my third oldest mate. "You woke up fast. Preston was coming to get you."

My emptiness surged, pressing to come out, to explode, but I held it down. I knew how this worked. Whatever this was inside of me, whatever had happened, this self-loathing, or hatred, or just utter exhaustion, didn't want me to have them back. Maybe I didn't feel I deserved them. Maybe it was whatever had gotten rid of the Omegas to begin with. I didn't know. I didn't care. It wasn't getting out; it wasn't taking this from me.

I was stronger.

"Kenzie." He wrapped his arms around me and held on for a second before he sagged. "I've been trying to get back."

He wasn't really up. Or he shouldn't have been yet. "I know."

"All right, brother." Rainer caught him when I would have dropped him. "Let's get you inside."

Jarret's head lolled back, hitting Rainer's shoulder. My oldest mate grinned at me. "Looks like we can tell why he wasn't doing well under the influence. He resisted. Tried to get back to you. Still is. How did he pull that shit off?"

I shook my head. I had no idea, but Jarret would never cease to surprise me. He really was strong and doing the constantly unexpected.

THE HOTEL ROOMS WERE NICE, clean, and there was a back entrance so we didn't have to walk past the front desk every time we went in and out. That was a benefit. Also, we'd been able to take up most of the rooms on one floor so all of the werewolves were together. I wanted to shift and run more than I wanted to breathe, but I couldn't, and longing for what couldn't be was as useful as stomping my foot at the moment.

Rainer had good reason for pausing our return. There would likely be no rest for the weary once we got to my swamp. I smiled. At this point, it was mine.

We had two connecting rooms, a door leading from one to the other. They were identical. I gave them a cursory glance before I wrapped my arms around Anton. If he was waiting to be brought back, I wasn't going to delay him any longer. It wasn't just my hands that burned but my entire body. That couldn't have been a good sign for how long this was going to take, or how much of my energy I would deplete in doing so.

Whatever it took, I'd bring him back.

I gripped his body, my wolf coming into my eyes. It looked like I really would need every ounce of my strength. A growl came out of my throat. I didn't go back to that place I could see, the wandering hallways where I'd been looking for Anton. No, this felt like a regular healing. I was Omega, and he was my wolf.

Only he was so much more than that. I turned my gaze to Rainer, to Preston, to the still unconscious Jarret. They were all mine. Above all else, what I wanted was them. Yes, revenge had to happen, which meant we had to figure out who had done this to us. Capture Brennan. Demand some answers. Find those in charge, and kill them like we had those in Georgia. We needed to do those things. There was also the absolute desire to cement werewolves back where we belonged—in packs, and shifting. But that had to wait, too.

All of that was important, yet not as dear to my heart as having the four of them back with me in Preston's unfurnished house in the swamp, with the slight tinge of sulfur in the air. Alligators floating by who could decide to walk up to our porch if they wanted to. Airboats buzzing on the water. Trucks driving up and down dirt roads. Falling apart mansions begging for people with vision to fix them.

I wanted to go home with these four men.

I wanted to wake up to Rainer's hand stroking my back even as he slept, like he had to actively touch me. I wanted to smell his food cooking. I needed to see Preston's easy smile as he woke everyone up in the mornings, because he was the only one with a real job. To hear him laugh, have his arms around me all night, to lie in my bed there and listen to him snore—as crazy as that was to desire. Jarret's voice as he spoke about his dreams, his ideas, his sweet kisses, and the way he looked at me like every time he saw me was the first time. I had to have those things like I required air to breathe.

And Anton, who was still lost and I would bring back now. I needed his forehead on my shoulder, his hand covering the place on my chest that held my heart, his unspoken words that somehow I heard. I would bring him back, and so fucking help me, I would hold onto them like my life depended on it. Because it did. I loved them completely. That was mating. That was everything.

I held onto him, a growl coming from my mouth. Rainer and Preston made eye contact. I could imagine what they thought—it was abnormal for me to do that—but right now, I had to give it everything. This was the only way I could reclaim my life. They were all mine.

If Anton could bring himself to feel his pain so acutely that I could fix it, then I wouldn't let him down. I was enough for this challenge. I always had been, it had just taken me almost losing everything to discover what I'd have automatically known in a kinder world.

I dug deep, and I let the Omega out. She howled.

I TWITCHED ON THE BED, my muscles moving of their own volition. My head pounded, and the empty inside of me surged like I'd never gotten two of my mating marks back.

I laughed to myself, a ridiculous sound given the circumstances, but there it was. I was full on drenched in sweat. Okay. I'd probably overdone it. In the future, I was going to keep a better rein on my powers. Just because I could douse the whole room in my energy, didn't mean I should do that.

The fact that Rainer and Preston were out cold on the floor was a good indication not to let loose like that again. This was a newfound ability. I'd been powerful, heady, and I'd fixed Anton, but now here I was. On my stomach with unconscious mates all around me, and no one to complain to about how badly I felt.

This time I giggled. Oh, I was such a perfect mess. Was that an oxymoron? *A perfect mess...*

A noise caught my attention, but I couldn't turn to look. I hadn't heard a door open, or noticed it anyway, so that meant it was a good chance that it was one of my guys getting up. The bed dipped, and strong hands gripped me before I was turned around.

Jarret's scent of the woods moved over me. It was a delayed reaction. I must have been really off. But, yes, the twitching. That was pretty obvious.

He pushed my hair off my forehead. "Kenzie?" His voice was low. "I've clearly missed something. Rainer and Preston are both snoring on the floor, and you're... obviously not okay." He kept his voice low, but his gaze traveled over me as he assessed my situation. If his nose was working properly, he might have some information about me from that, too.

"I fixed Anton. I overdid it, but it's been a struggle." I was so happy to see Jarret. I wished I could make my hand work and touch him. "You can't know how glad I am to see you."

He kissed the end of my nose. "Been trying to get back to you. I fought and fought the compulsion."

That made sense. "They had you somewhere where people weren't doing well. I guess you found a way to sort of resist. That's impressive, Jarret."

"Nonsense." He shook his head. "I didn't pull out. That would have maybe been impressive. All I did was try and fail. Tell me what I can do for you."

That was a very good question, and not one I had an answer for, per se. "I've been in bad shape. Better since Preston and Rainer came back. But, no, things have not been going well. I need... I can get into the explanation of it later, but do you think you could mark me? It really could help."

He tilted his head, the wolf showing up for a second before it vanished. Jarret tugged down my shirt to look at my neck area. "I can, and then when you're better, you can tell me why mine is gone."

I nodded, which seemed to be the only movement I could control. "Sure. I promise."

He smoothed my shirt away, gently. As I watched his teeth changed to fangs, he bit down hard right on his spot. My body bucked beneath him as he lapped at the wound with his tongue. The empty didn't like it, shrinking, but it was the least of my concerns at that moment. Jarret's bite didn't correct my power drain.

I loved having the sense of him back, the feel of Jarret. It was calming, which was funny since he'd been so often accused of being anxious before he met me. Jarret was steady, he kept me firm, got me grounded. Kept me present.

He lifted his head, his fangs receding. "Didn't fix it, did it?"

"Helped in other ways. I have an empty inside of me.

Hard to explain. It keeps trying to take over. Your marks... they help." I wasn't sure how else to explain it.

He laid his body on top of mine. I sighed. It was comforting. The heat. The pressure. The way he was just lying there on top of me.

"I overdid it. I think this is just a result of that. It'll stop. I hope."

"I bet you fixed the problems of everyone in a three-mile radius." His grin was fast. "Just lie here. Don't do anything else. We have nowhere to be, nothing to do."

I shook my head. "You really have no way of knowing that. We could be hiding in this hotel room because we're hiding from the Loch Ness Monster."

He lifted one eyebrow. "Well, if Nessie shows up, I'll shift and challenge her. Still, I don't see any lakes around. I may not be up on all my mythology, but my education did include classical studies and historical mythos. I could..."

I giggled, and he stopped. "No, keep going."

"You're totally making fun of me."

"No, I'm loving it. You're distracting me. Go on. How will you take on the monster?"

He kissed my neck right above where he'd marked me. I shuddered. Heat flooded me. I couldn't follow through with what I wanted, not right then. But I loved the sensation. "I'm good with things that might not be real. With things that are... maybe not real. See? I met this beautiful girl, and somehow, she smelled like mine. She lets me spend time with her. Over and over she fixed me. I think she probably saved my life, even though I can't remember it."

I tilted my head. I was tired. The adrenaline must be hitting now. My hand shook, but I could raise it. I stroked my finger down his face. "I missed you so much."

He kissed me lightly. "Me, too. So much. I couldn't think, but I... longed for you."

My eyes were closing, once again something out of my control. "I am going to fall asleep. I'm sorry. I don't want to be rude and just start snoring."

He kissed my lips gently. "You never snore. Go to sleep. I'll take care of things here. The Loch Ness Monster or elves or whatever happens. I love, love, love you."

I OPENED my eyes to three werewolves staring down at me. Rainer smiled at Jarret. "Told you she was waking. The cute little noises stopped."

I rubbed my face. "Hi. You guys are okay."

"Oh." Preston rocked back on his feet. "We know. We could all run to the Texas border and back if we wanted to right now. I've never been stronger. And everyone is fixed. Yes, everyone. Some of them are still out cold, recovering, but they're all fixed. You exploded with power. I mean... fuck."

Jarret sat down next to me, kissing my neck as he breathed me in. "You guys didn't see her. I get that it's cool. But, I'm here to tell you—she does that again, and she might just die."

I wrapped my arms around his neck. "I'm okay. I made it, Jarret. It's what I do. With you guys to help me, I can survive. I can do what I need to. My wolf is scary strong. I'll learn how to temper it."

He didn't say anything, and I didn't know if that was a good thing or a bad thing. All I knew was that it was wonderful to have him right there in my arms and be able to hold him. "I didn't have any nightmares. No dreams. No visits. It was just quiet."

Maybe Jarret had been filled in, because he didn't question that. Instead, he ran his finger down the spot where his mark was. "Lots of protection to keep you safe. In sleep and awake. Anton will be up soon. Then we'll all be back together. And fuck the world, no one is separating us again."

"Amen to that." Preston stretched, showing his belly slightly when his shirt came up. I grinned. Little moments. They really mattered, and ogling my guys was going to be a favorite past time.

Still, we had serious things to discuss. "After we get things settled at home, we need to find Brennan. Drag him in. Get answers. One way or another."

"Sounds almost brutal." Jarret kissed my cheek.

"Nothing almost about it, Brother." Rainer extended his hand, and I took it. "She's one of us. You should have seen her managing what we had to do to get you out of there like it was nothing at all. She's a wolf. We protect our pack. Period. Someone tried to neuter us all these years. The Accords, that's all they were. A way to keep us from being us. But I feel fantastic. And, yes, time to get Brennan to drop his corporate hunters story. Time to know who we get to kill."

All of their eyes turned wolf, and I squirmed a little bit. What's more, I knew they could smell it. I smiled. "The idea of taking out our enemies to protect our pack?" I bit my lip. "It's really fucking hot."

NINE

Preston elbowed Rainer. "Let's go get the vehicle ready. We're like the clown car, except instead of clowns, we have werewolves. I'll carry Anton out the backdoor. Someone is going to notice and think we're hauling bodies."

Rainer shook his head. "Be really difficult to explain this to the cops. Trust me, I've already been on the wrong side of the law."

Jarret watched them exit into the other room, and a few minutes later, there was a clicking noise as the door opened and closed, signaling they were leaving the room. He turned back to me. "You scared me last night. I tried to fake calm, and I don't think you were particularly scenting things, or you'd have known that."

I sat all the way up, wrapping my arms around him. "It's been a hard time. I keep coming to an edge, and then finding out there is still another edge for me to reach. At one point, an Alpha of a town we stumbled on suggested I was dying." I met Jarret's gaze head on. "I might have been. But I'm not now. I can't promise not to scare you again, because I keep freaking myself the fuck out, too."

He pushed me back on the bed, coming over me like he had last night but this time there was no gentle to it. I reached up and bit his bottom lip. Jarret's eyes turned wolf, and he smirked at me, licking the blood where I'd nipped him.

"You're being bad this morning."

"I don't know. This feels very, very good."

He nodded. "It does."

We kissed, our lips fusing together until I couldn't tell where he started and I ended. Our clothes came off. Had we ripped them? Thrown them? I wasn't sure. I just knew we'd managed to get naked, fast. I turned my hands into claws and dug them into his back. He jerked and growled against my mouth as his hips pushed into me.

He pulled back to adore me with his eyes. "Do that any time you want. Mark me everywhere. Tear me up and leave scars."

"Maybe not that dramatic." My empty was practically gone. Euphoria at being with Jarret flooded me. I grinned from ear-to-ear. "You're mine. You know that, right?"

His smile widened. "I'd better be. Not sure what I'd do with myself if I weren't." He kissed me hard, and I sighed against him. The mood changed, seriousness taking over the moment. When I opened my eyes, he stared down at me. "When you make that noise, it does something to me in a way that makes me feel like the most powerful male on the planet. I am the reason you made that sound... it's fucking heaven."

When he dropped his head again, it wasn't to kiss my mouth, it was to make love to my skin everywhere else. Everywhere Jarret could reach with his lips, he did. When I shivered and moaned again, he spent a lot of time on that spot—right where my neck met my shoulder.

Jarret followed his trail of kisses with gentle, teasing licks. This was new for me, and my already hot, wet, pussy got even more heated. I squirmed beneath him. I tried to hold onto him, but he was moving, and it wasn't steady, so instead, I grabbed onto the bed. Yes, this was just what I wanted. I knew how awful it was not to have him, and I didn't ever want to lose it. Finally, he came back to my spot, moving past it this time to kiss me all over his mark.

"No matter what happens," he whispered against my skin, not even raising his gaze to meet my own. "This stays right here. This is my spot, and you are my mate. I'm always with you, even if I can't be."

I nodded. Yes, no matter what happened, I wouldn't lose it again. My empty—that part of me that always felt less than—couldn't have it. Ever.

Jarret lifted his head to kiss my chin. "How is it that I can never get enough of you? The more I have, the more I want."

Before he kissed me again, he ran his finger from my chin all the way down to my pussy. I shuddered. "You're so hot there. The place I'm about to touch. Men have written great literature in their awe of your female places. It's like my little piece of heaven."

Jarret groaned, and I stared up at him. "I'm not the only one who makes great noises."

He didn't smile, instead, he kissed down my body in the direction that his finger had gone. I arched my back. This was too much. I wouldn't have believed it, but there was such a thing, it turned out, as too much lead up. I dripped, I ached. I wanted fulfillment, the connection with Jarret that said we were fully back together. The waiting was sweet torture I wasn't sure I could live through.

Still, Jarret wasn't done with me. He didn't finish his

trail of making me needy by touching my core. Instead, he moved back upward, taking my breast in his mouth. He bit down on my nipple. My whole body throbbed with need.

His breathing was rough as he tongued my nipple, bringing it to a peak, letting it go, and then doing it again. I panted.

"Jarret," I finally begged. "You're killing me."

He shook his head. "I'm loving you."

I reached between us, grasping his cock in my hand. He jerked when I gave him a long stroke. Jarret flared his nostrils. "Careful with that. I may not remember the time apart, but my body is fully aware that I haven't been inside of you in too long."

I arched an eyebrow. "Torture goes both ways, my love."

"All right, Mate, point made." He flipped me over.

I raised my eyebrows. This was a new way for us. Not that I would complain. Everything with Jarret always ended up fantastic. This would, too. I looked over my shoulder at him. "Wanting a new position?"

"I want all of the positions with you." He moved behind me, pressing his fingers inside of me for a second. I clenched around him, and he moaned. Jarret took an audible breath. I smiled. He must have really wanted to scent me right there. Maybe I should have been embarrassed, but I wasn't. Not even a little bit.

He stroked my clit, and I cried out. Foreplay was wonderful, except I really didn't need it. "Jarret..."

"I know." He kissed my shoulder. "I just love touching you. It's such a privilege to get to do so."

With those words, he pressed inside of me. I cried out. My muscles drew him in and clenched around him, so that I practically sheathed him like a glove. I grabbed onto the headboard harder, already knowing I was going to need the support. From this angle, he could really get deep inside of me, and when he pulled out to press back in, I discovered the other benefit: Jarret could hit my spot with every pass like this.

I closed my eyes. Oh yes, this was heaven. It just was. Sweat broke out on my body. He squeezed my breast as he pulled out and then back into me. I shuddered. I'd never known it was possible to ache like this, to need so much more. To have my body actually demand completion like it was as essential as breathing.

Jarret's breaths were strained like mine, and soon we were a chorus of moans and gasps. I loved how he sounded. I closed my eyes to hold onto this moment. The way it felt, how it was like we existed alone in the universe for just those seconds.

But too soon and also not quick enough, pleasure overtook me. I let go of the headboard and fell back against him. He grabbed onto me, holding me to his chest while I shattered. Jarret wasn't far behind me. Maybe it was seconds. He shouted my name.

We jolted together, the aftershocks of pleasure that was more than just lovemaking but also a reclaiming, rocked me to my core. I smiled, unable to breathe, but so happy. I had my mate back.

And I was never letting him go again.

WE WALKED hand-in-hand to the RV. What I really wanted to do was sleep, but it wasn't that I was tired, more like I had a case of the cuddles after what Jarret and I had just shared. I wanted to snuggle and doze in his arms.

That wasn't on the agenda, but I hoped that someday soon it would be again.

The door flung open as we approached, and Preston poked his head out. "Oh good. You two are here. Come on, Jarret. Come meet our mother-in-law."

I gasped. In all the... getting reacquainted, I'd completely forgotten that my mother was among the people who we'd saved. I let go of Jarret's hand and rushed inside just as my mother rose. People surrounded us. It was hard to even find somewhere to stand lest I bang into someone.

"Omega," several people said, and one person grabbed onto my pant leg. I wasn't sure what that was about. I only had eyes for my mother. She stared at me with her mouth open before she reached out and hugged me tightly.

"Kenzie," she whispered in my ear. "You're okay."

We'd never had that much hugging in our relationship. It wasn't that we weren't close; it was more like my mother was lost. The Accords had taken a huge chunk of her soul, and I could always tell she was blocked from us. But even with the strain that was always there for us, there wasn't anything quite as wonderful as being hugged by my mother when I didn't feel well.

"You saved everyone. How are you the Omega? How did we not know?"

The RV jolted forward, and people groaned.

"Sorry," Isaac called back.

My mother pulled back and grinned at me. "And you mated the Lejeunes. How did that happen?"

Lots of hows going on here, and I had no answers. "You met Rainer and Preston. This is Jarret. And Anton is..."

Rainer pointed behind him. "Out cold on the bed. All of the people with him are still sleeping. Everyone else is up and healthy."

My hands didn't burn. That was a very good sign. At least for now, these people were healthy. My mother shook Jarret's hand, saying hello. She'd been taken while I was kidnapped and woken up to four sons-in-law and me the Omega. It had to be sort of surreal.

All at once, everyone started talking, and it seemed like they all wanted my attention. Thanks. Omega. Questions. All at once. I staggered backward, and Preston caught me.

"Easy." He wrapped his arms around me and brought us both down to the empty seat on the couch. His touch helped. Having my mother here really made the changes in me feel more obvious. I didn't used to be this sensitive to people being around. Now it was like they ate away at me.

"Hey," Jarret barked to the room. "Everyone tone it down. She doesn't like the attention, doesn't want the thanks, and forcing it on her is draining as hell. Use your noses. All of you have an aware wolf now. Does she smell happy to you?"

Everyone quieted down, and guilt flooded me. They hadn't really been doing anything wrong. "I know that you're all grateful, and I am so glad I could help you. I drain easily. It might be something that will get better with time. I've been an Omega for... what... two months?"

"Two and a half." Rainer winked at me. "Want to go sit with Anton? Have a breather?"

"You've been an Omega your whole life," Gus called out from across the room. "You've been allowed to practice it for two and a half months. What you're feeling isn't just from using your natural powers, but from having not been allowed to use them for so long. What we don't do or say can be as draining on us as anything else."

Rainer grinned. "Well, now that we're all thoroughly chastised..."

Gus laughed, throwing his head back. "I wondered if you'd ever develop a mouth on you."

Rainer ignored him, looking back at my mom. "Ma'am, I feel obligated to tell you that I've been to jail. I have a record. You may or may not already know that."

Yep, I was going to go sit with Anton.

THE RV TOOK A SHARP LEFT, and I fell off the bed, managing to grab onto Anton just in time to stop him from doing the same. I rubbed at my arm. My elbow had taken most of the hit. Up front, everyone shouted, and I rushed forward to see what the fuss was about.

We'd turned onto a quieter highway, heading toward home about half-an-hour before but now, in front of us, were five men with guns. They were pointed at our RV.

"They're wolves," my brother shouted out to the group.

Rainer rushed toward the front. "I don't care. Run them the fuck over."

"Hold on," I answered fast. "Rainer, smell that. I can taste the metal even here. We can help them."

"Not while they're pointing guns anywhere in the general direction of you."

Suddenly, it was like the world tilted sideways. I didn't know how else to describe what happened to me, as though I took a step outside of myself and instead of being in the RV with all the other wolves, I walked down a long hallway. Similar to, but not exactly like, the one I'd been in with Anton.

A man stood, staring at me. He was tall, silver haired, and his eyes were all wolf. "Omega."

I looked around. What in the ever-loving fuck was going

on? My language had regressed, but I'd reached a threshold of messed up that polite discourse could no longer adequately manage.

"What is going on?" I sniffed the air, but I could smell nothing. This wasn't real. It was like Anton's hallucinations or my dreams of other werewolves. This guy was alive, somewhere, but not currently with me.

He walked toward me. "It's amazing how little humans understand wolves, isn't it? I mean... they think they do. Behavioral scientists have big statements, and the memes make their way around the Internet. But the truth is, they really don't get it, do they?"

This guy wanted to talk about human beings' lack of understanding about wolves? "I'm not sure how much they do or don't understand. As far as what they know about us, we're legends to them. They don't think we're real, and I'd rather keep it that way."

"Not me." He shook his head. I couldn't touch him. He was a projection, a telepathic joining, but not in the current spot with me. "I want the humans to know all about us. After we're all dead. Like we're some kind of specimen in a museum."

I waited for him to laugh or indicate in any way that he was kidding, because he had to be. I blinked rapidly. "You want us to be... fossils?" I couldn't deal with that. "Are you... are you sick?"

"I was sick." He walked away from me. "For a very long time. And none of you Omegas would help me. Ever. So I stopped being sick, and now... I'm a god."

It couldn't be a good thing to have someone call themselves a god. Particularly when they were able to form a mental link with me that pulled me into a dream state in the middle of an attack during the day.

I had to put aside the lunacy of what he'd said and focus on the other bits. None of the Omegas would help him.

"Look, I don't know any other Omegas. It's just me. And if I can help you, then I will, but I must tell you that you don't look sick to me."

He laughed, throwing his head back. "I did. For the longest time I looked sick, like a monster. People would shriek, they would cry, they would run. My pack abandoned me to the madness. And then one day, it stopped. I was this again," he pointed to himself, "and I had clarity. I could see that the problem was that we existed at all. I got rid of the Omegas. So easy to do. But it begs the question, how are you here, Omega? When you never should have been born at all."

I jolted back into myself. The door to the RV slammed open, and my fellow wolves streamed out, shifting as they went. I caught my breath. Rainer barked orders, and Preston grabbed the wheel from my brother, backing the RV up. They argued about something. Jarret ran out the door, shifting mid-stride as he jumped out of the moving vehicle.

My breath caught in my throat. I had been gone minutes, but no one had known. We were being attacked, and maybe it was possible that the man who had managed to hijack my consciousness and claimed to have killed the Omegas had something to do with this.

Those were all things I was going to have to deal with later. For now, there were wolves on the highway, humans bound to notice, and this whole thing was a clusterfuck of epic proportions. Preston was trying to get us away, but that was the last thing I needed right now.

My mother shouted at me, and I hated to disobey what I knew Rainer wanted. Guns fired, and my body burned with unused energy. I shifted, my body becoming a wolf. Somehow, I had to figure out how to be a wolf every day, regardless of circumstances. Staying human too long killed our souls. As a people, we knew this, and yet we forced the shifts down regularly, even without the Accords.

"MacKenzie," Rainer's voice was low, like he was mid-shift himself. "Don't do that."

I jumped out the door, hitting the street with a thump. Pop. Pop. Pop. The controlled wolves were firing human guns. We'd done that ourselves to get Preston, but those had been tranqs. I could smell the bullets as they left those guns. They were not as harmless as what we'd done.

Two of our people were down. The wolves who had been shooting at us were overwhelmed. That was good news, but as I sniffed the air, I knew none of us were supposed to be this way. This had been done to us. Wolves were not natural allies, people disliked each other, werewolves didn't get along. But this? This was abhorrent, and if I was alone in the world to fix it, then so be it.

One of the downed wolves rose, lifting the gun again. Oh, no. He wasn't going to shoot any of my people. I launched myself at him. I'd fix him eventually, but that didn't mean I wasn't going to hurt him a little first. I tore into his arm, yanking it back until he yelped and let go of the gun.

Jarret growled at me, biting down on the man's arm and knocking me back so that I was behind him. His gaze said it all. He wasn't happy with me.

With the man's blood in my mouth, I threw out my power. All of it. Like I had done accidentally when I'd healed Anton. This time it was purposeful, and standing in my fur helped. I was stronger as my wolf.

A growl sounded through the night. It was Rainer, but as I turned to look, Anton tore out of the RV, which had stopped on the side of the road. Rainer was right behind him, and Preston closely following. I was going to be in a serious amount of trouble later, but I couldn't say that I particularly cared right then. The wolves stopped fighting, overwhelmed by my power. Unlike earlier, it didn't knock down everyone. Was that because we were all wolves right now?

A female wolf howled in distress, and I turned slightly. That was my mother. I'd never seen her as a wolf before. We looked similar, which was interesting because we really didn't in our human forms.

I huffed. Anton strode over to me, growling at the unconscious wolves. I turned toward my people who had been shot. They were all okay, bullets gone from their bodies.

I rubbed up against my finally-awake mate. He knocked me with his head, which was as much to move me along as anything else.

Fine. I'd go. Wolves started shifting back. I was glad they'd had the sense, considering there was not a backup on the highway, and we might have eyes on us any second. Whatever the humans could see, it must have looked confusing. A bunch of dogs? I didn't know. Were we going to suffer for this?

I guessed only time would tell.

Should we have just run over the men?

ANTON STILL HADN'T SPOKEN to me by the time we got to our house. Not that he could ever speak, but he hadn't tried to have any moment with me at all. In fact, he wouldn't make eye contact. I met Rainer's gaze. He was pissed, not trying to hide it, and I was sure I was about to get an earful, but he wasn't pretending that he couldn't see me. I supposed I should thank him for that.

The RV was quiet, buzzing with whispers if anything at all. My mother sat up front, talking to Isaac.

"All right." I spoke in the general direction of Preston and Jarret, who didn't seem angry at me. Although there was so much acrid tension in the air, it was hard to tell who was mad at whom. Or maybe everyone in the RV was mad at me for daring to stop the fight and heal everyone. "We're here."

Rainer rose. "We are."

Isaac opened the door, and without another word, Rainer bounded out, followed by Anton. I leaned back in my seat. This wasn't how I'd pictured going home.

Preston put a hand on my knee. "Rainer doesn't do scared well."

I swallowed. Tears threatened to spill, but I was going to wait until I was alone. "I'm sorry I frightened him. But what about Anton? He's being cold."

"I don't know. Hard to tell sometimes what's in his head. You read him better than anyone, but part of the silence is if he doesn't want you to know, there's no way to make him communicate. Maybe he got scared, too."

Jarret offered me his hand. "Come on. I smell so many wolves here, it's reminding me of when we were really little. Maybe that's made up in my head. I was really young. But, it's like it was, somehow."

Preston nodded. "You're not wrong. When we were young, this whole bayou was filled with us. It was like always being home."

"Did I do wrong?"

My mother stopped, putting her hand on my shoulder.

"What would any of us do if something happened to you? I'm your mother. When you were taken, I wanted to dissolve into a puddle of pain. But, what will everyone do now?"

I had to tell them all about the vision I'd had. Yet, there was so much wrong here, I couldn't talk about it like this. Not when I felt two inches tall.

TEN

The house was packed. I needed to talk to Miranda, but not until I had a chance to fix things with my guys. They always came first. The problem was finding them. I had unconscious wolves, ones rocking in corners, others snarling in cages. Family members who wanted hugs, and stepping into the living room only reminded me head on this was where Kevin had died. I swallowed. We needed to do something to remember him, for all of us. My gaze fell on my mother-in-law, she sat in Gus' lap. She hadn't had much to say, and I couldn't blame her.

Today probably felt like the day after Kevin had died for her.

I put my hand on Jarret's arm. "Could you talk to your mom about doing a memorial for Kevin? Just the family and those who knew him. We can do a bigger one mourning all those who have been lost with something later."

He blinked rapidly. "I can do that. Yes. I haven't... I haven't really let myself think about that."

"I know. But she is." I nodded toward her. "And we all need to. In about an hour, can you and Preston, wherever he is—I think he might be hiding from the crowd—Anton, and Rainer meet me outside. By the house where we first battled The Loups."

He scratched his head. "I don't really remember that. Shifting fog."

"Preston will. Thanks, my love. I have to find Anton or Rainer. I may have one of them with me when I meet you at the house."

He touched my arm. "Have one of them, or wait for me. Don't go alone."

"I won't. Trust me, I'm not going to do anything foolish again." I kissed his cheek. "I love you."

His skin was warm where I pressed my lips to it. I breathed him in. "Any idea where Anton or Rainer go when they're mad?"

Jarret shook his head. "I know there are a lot of scents here, but you're going to have to follow your nose. We didn't live here long enough for Anton to develop a place, and I don't remember if Rainer had a hideout."

That made sense. "See you in just a bit."

I sniffed the air. The house was permeated with the smells of everyone. I wasn't in love with it. This was our space. Funny how I could suddenly get possessive when I'd hardly lived here long enough for me to call it mine.

I could find my guys anywhere. Anton was upstairs. Rainer was on the back porch. I didn't know what was wrong with Anton, but I did with Rainer, so I turned that way first. Rainer leaned against the back wall, watching rain come down onto the swamp. I stood there for a second, and I watched it. We must have just missed the downpour coming in.

The pings were slow, it wasn't a deluge of water, just a few drops followed by a few others. They pinged as they hit the water, creating a circle in the swamp before dissipating into nothingness. I walked toward Rainer. He turned slightly to look at me.

"I'm cooling off."

I waved my hand. "In this heat?"

"MacKenzie..."

I cut him off. "I'm sorry."

He opened and closed his mouth. "Well, fuck. How am I supposed to stay mad at you, if you go and do that?"

I put out my hand, and he took it, drawing me to him. "Listen to me, Mate, I can't protect you if you don't listen to me."

I nodded. "Something happened right before the fight, it's not an excuse, but I need to explain it. To all of you in just a bit. I asked Jarret to get your brothers and meet me by the house where we first fought the Loups."

He scrunched up his face. "We were in the RV, what could have happened?"

"A lot, actually. My only other excuse is there was a fight, and well... my wolf side likes it. I know I'm the Omega, and I'm supposed to stay away from things, behind closed doors. I get it, I—"

He shook his head. "You are supposed to stay safe because you're my mate. Because I love you. Because I've already let you down. I want you to stay back and not fight, because your super-duper Omega power fails sometimes. You can't count on it. You're getting stronger, but it almost killed you. Sometimes we have to let the other person be who they are supposed to be. I do that with you. You are practically draining yourself dry, and I don't stop you. I get that you're the Omega. You have to understand that the four of us were made to fight. We're alpha werewolves, all four of us. Oh sure, they listen to me. For now. But mark my words, they could easily take over."

I had a feeling he'd lost track. That was okay. We all needed to be able to go where we needed to go sometimes. Did anyone really ever let Rainer talk? Just ramble?

He continued. "The point is that I need you to let us do what we do. We take care of you, and we destroy enemies who hurt our pack. Yes, you can fight, but you don't always have to."

I swallowed. "Okay. I'm sorry. I will... do better." I dropped my eyes. In this moment, there was no question that we had a hierarchy, and he was Alpha. Sure, it was screwed up because I wasn't an everyday wolf, but the feelings of not wanting to disappoint him were there, and it went beyond normal boundaries. It was everything I could do not to drop to my knees and beg...

In fact, the thought no sooner hit me than I decided to...

"No." He grabbed onto my arm. "I can smell it. Where you fall into the regular wolf dynamics. Your wolf knows it, too. Maybe part of it makes you feel safe, secure? I don't know. It comes on all of a sudden, but it goes away when you have to be the Omega. I don't need any additional apologies." He drew me to him even tighter, pressing his mouth to mine. He was warm, and he tasted like home. I closed my eyes and let him ravage my mouth. This was Rainer. He was *mine*. Soon, he stopped, staring into my eyes. "Go make it right with Anton. We need to all be back together. Figure out some strategy. Then let you fix the mess in that house right now."

I stroked my thumb down his nose. He grinned at me. "Go. Before I say I don't care that we have an audience of wolves I don't know in the next room and fuck you on this porch."

I loved that idea, but I did need to see what was wrong with Anton. He was still missing from my soul. If he was hurt, I needed to know. And, I owed him a million apologies as well. I'd really let him down.

"Thanks for forgiving me like that."

He smirked. "Would have been a lot harder if you'd gotten hurt instead of flooring the enemy. See you in an hour."

I left him and headed back into the house. Miranda stepped in front of me. "I can see that you have a lot going on. But what should we do with those we rescued?"

"I need to take care of my people. When I'm done, I'm going to eat something." My stomach rumbled at the thought, but it would need to wait until later. "And then I'll fix everyone."

She nodded. "This is remarkable what you've done. I've never known an Omega to do what you've been able to."

"Thanks. We all do what we have to. I might prefer to have a team of other Omegas stationed around the world handling local issues as opposed to this broad sweep I'm doing." When had I started to use words like that? Broad sweep? I sounded like something I'd hear on television. Or a podcast. Not coming out of my mouth. Internally, I shrugged. What did it matter?

I took the stairs two at a time and finally found my way to Anton.

He sat in the dark, his head in his hands, and I walked to him quickly. This was his room. The others all had someone in them, so he'd either thrown everyone out or he'd just been lucky it remained empty.

"Hi." He had to know I was there, so saying it seemed like the right thing to do.

He lifted his head but that was the only acknowledgment I was going to get. I walked closer, dropping down onto my knees in front of where he sat. "Anton, I'm not sure what you're angry about, but if it's what I think it is, please let me apologize."

He dropped his hand from his face and stared at me for a long moment before he shook his head. I could usually read him so well, but I was getting nothing right now. Just the scent of anger and pain. I had to try again.

"I let you down. It's my job as an Omega to fix what is wrong. I've been doing it over and over again. You're my mate. They'd hurt you, scarred you so deep inside that I couldn't tell, and they took you because I'm lousy at this. Please forgive me. I'm never going to stop feeling like I—"

His hand shot out so fast I never saw it coming, but when he placed it on top of my lips, he was gentle about it. Was that the Anton equivalent of telling me to hush?

I stared up at him. He met my gaze for a long moment. Eventually, he let go of my lips and placed both his hands over his chest. He patted it twice. I swallowed. "Sweetheart, I'm not sure what you're saying."

He looked all around and then back at me. That much I'd understood. "I don't know where the tablet is. I don't remember where it was before it all went to hell, and I have no idea what happened since. Did Brennan and his people go through here? I... I really don't know."

Anton nodded and then got to his feet. He looked around for a second before he rushed over to his desk. After pulling out a pencil and a notebook he started to write fast. He walked over to me and handed me the page he'd ripped out.

This is my fault. All of it. I did this to all of us.

I read what he wrote twice. Then a third time before I met his gaze. "How can this be your fault? You were a baby.

They came, and they took you. Hurt you. Triggered something in you. I have a theory as to why and how. It's not your fault. This happened to you, not because of you."

He wrote again. *None of this would have happened if I'd just somehow resisted.*

I grabbed his hand and pressed it to my heart. "Anton, no one knows better than me how it feels to think I'm responsible for something that is not actually my fault." I let go of his hand to pull down the neck of my shirt. "See that?"

I saw the second his gaze narrowed on where his bite should have been.

I talked fast before he made assumptions. "In a move I couldn't explain if I tried, I let myself get so guilt-ridden and angry at myself for losing all of you, for being responsible for this, that I made my mate marks go away. It nearly killed me. By the time Preston got to me—out of his mind, and trying to capture or kill me—I was running on fumes. I might have died if not for his return. Bit-by-bit, you guys are helping me to reclaim my strength. So, I get it Anton. But don't let this terrible scenario do that to you. My love, you've been through enough."

He wrapped me up in his arms. His heart beat fast beneath my ear. His shoulders sagged, and I hoped that meant he understood, that he accepted what I'd said to him. He pulled back just a little to look at me, moving my shirt again so he could look at the marks.

Anton ran his hands over his brothers' marks, raising his eyebrow to me. I understood his unasked question, which was so wonderful since it seemed like I'd lost my knack to do so. "Yes, please, give me back yours. I... I had something happen just a little while ago; I'll explain when we meet up with the others. I just don't want to say it again and again, and anyway, yes. I miss your mark. I can feel its absence like you're not quite here with me yet."

He tapped my chin, and I looked into his eyes. They turned wolf for a second before they went back to their calm depths. Yes, he was here with me. I caught my breath. I'd never been so grateful to be in a moment than I was right then.

"Bite me now. Please."

He nodded once before his teeth elongated in his mouth. We were always in such crisis or in such a hurry, that I took no time to admire the magic of what we could do. Right then and there, he'd partially shifted just because he wanted to. I touched the end of his fang with my thumb, feeling the sting for a second, and grinned at him.

"Do it."

He smoothed his thumb over the spot, sending shivers through my body.

Anton bit down. I cried out, first from the pain, but then from the pleasure that followed. There was such a feeling of completeness—of at last being right—that euphoria flooded my system. I sagged against him as he continued to lick the spot with his tongue.

"Thank you." I choked on the words. I'd never felt so lucky in my life. I'd gotten him back. I'd saved all of them. "So help me, I won't lose you again."

He lifted his head, licking his lips to take the few drops of my blood off of them. His fangs vanished. I grabbed onto his shirt, yanking it down so I could see my own mark there. I placed my palm over it.

The next second, I was against the wall. I wrapped my arms around his neck. He kissed me, hard. That was the only foreplay I was going to get and that was fine by me. I creamed my panties. Oh God, yes, I wanted him. *Badly*.

He yanked down my pants, and they fell down to the floor. My underwear came next. They got hooked on my feet, not making it over my shoes, and I couldn't bring myself to care.

I cupped his erection on the outside of his pants. He flared his nostrils before he dropped his own pants and underwear. It hadn't taken him long. Anton wanted me and badly.

"Miss me?"

His smile was huge before he kissed me again. I pushed my tongue into his mouth, and he tugged on the end of my hair. The bite of pain fueled me forward.

Anton pressed inside of me. He'd been a gentle lover the first time we'd been together. Caring, careful. This was different. This was a claiming. This was him letting me know that I was his. They'd all been like this in the reclaiming. I needed it just as much. We'd been violently separated, and we were coming back together like we might not get the chance again.

He jerked inside of me, and my muscles clenched. Anton reached between us. It was awkward, but he managed to stick his fingers where I needed them to be while he pressed in and pulled out. Anton found my clit and rubbed. The sensation was incredible. This was rough. Dirty. Awkward. And so fucking hot, I almost couldn't believe it.

I bit down on his lip, and he grunted. It was so unusual to hear sound from Anton, that when I heard anything it amazed me. Even that small noise was a lot. We banged against the wall, and I dug my fingers into his back, clawing at his shirt. I might have growled. Who knew what was happening anymore? I closed my eyes and held on.

Then I was coming. Hard. I yelled, uncaring who heard

or what happened in the future. There was just this, there was just now. Anton was back. He was mine, and as he emptied himself inside of me, I'd never felt so alive, so full, or so complete.

I kissed both his cheeks, holding him while he shook. "I've got you."

It seemed foolish to say that while he held me against the wall. It was quite clear he had me and not the other way around, and yet I wanted him to know it. I'd have him. Forever and ever.

THE RAIN that started earlier had gotten heavier, then lighter, then disappeared, and now it was back to drizzling. We could go inside the abandoned house. But I was happy standing outside. The heat seemed to rise from the ground as though the water coming down on it made it stronger, more intense as it rose.

My skin itched. I wanted to shift. Now that I had all four of them back, all I wanted was a good romp through the swamp with my guys as we ran on all fours. That wasn't going to happen, but going inside was probably only going to make it worse.

I'd rather be wet.

"Right before the battle, I had an experience. I'm not quite sure how to explain it. The closest I could explain is that it was like what happened to me when I'd dream before Rainer came back." I looked at Preston. He was the only one who was going to really get what I meant. "I would be transported somewhere and talk to a werewolf who needed help. I couldn't help them, and I'd wake up feeling sick. Worse than when I'd gone to bed."

Preston nodded. "Thirty-two minutes of sleep total. Over and over again. It was killing her. But when Rainer came back, two marks seemed to offer more protection in her sleep. What are you saying? It happened again? You were awake."

"I know." I swallowed. "A man came. He drew me to him. I stood there, and then I wasn't in my body anymore. None of you had any idea. We talked. He wants to kill all wolves, expose us as fossils... He was sick. I could feel it, like with those other wolves. But he looked fine except in the eyes. Guys, I can't explain it. It was like he was a Loup. But not a Loup."

Anton crossed his arms over his chest. He wasn't happy, but he didn't have answers.

Jarret scrunched up his face. "He drew your consciousness to him? How is that even possible?"

"Well..." This was where I started to have theories. "We're all connected psychically. I think that's been proven over and over. A wolf thing. I've got the connection with the Omega, but it's to everyone, really. That's why you all went down when they came for us. Piece-by-piece. Like dominoes. But... what if there was one mind, one Alpha mind that could reach all of us, control us, that would explain things. That's how he gets in there to begin with. Infects the whole link. And Brennan was able to trigger the response with that high-pitched noise, like it was waiting for it."

"Interesting." Rainer took two steps toward me. He looked me up and down as though he wanted to make sure for himself that I was okay. "And if that mind was sick..."

"It could be a disaster. An Alpha mind... we know they exist. You have to have one to run a pack. Miranda. Rainer." He shook his head, but I ignored it. "Any of the natural

Alphas. And one stronger than the rest, but rather than be benign or a leader who cares, he's psychotic."

"Hidden like a human. Living in the world. Mind like a Loup. No Omegas around." Preston sighed. "It's a true recipe for a disaster. I wonder... remember that name I heard when I was under that I sort of remember? Ross Morgan. We should find out if it's him. The doctors mentioned him."

Rainer nodded. "I still can't believe you have memories. It's a blank for me. And the fact that Jarret found some way to resist. It's amazing."

Anton tilted his head. I could understand his thoughts. He wanted to know what we were supposed to do about any of this.

I cleared my throat. "We go get Brennan. He's the only one who would have answers. His corporation discussion was bullshit. That wasn't corporate where we were. They're not making money researching product. This is not the work of four former Hunters. It's a cover story, and a bad one. I know it." I sniffed the air. "Like I know the rain is about to get worse."

Sure enough, the water pressure increased. We'd be drenched soon.

Rainer looked at all four of us. "Preston, go get Brennan. Pick three people to go with you. Not us. I have to stay here in case something happens, and I don't want Jarret or Anton to leave. I want our Omega to have three of her four mates here with her. Protection. If this Ross is getting into her head, then I'm not going to rest easy until he's contained."

Preston's eyes went wolf. "I won't fail. Brennan and anyone with him will be mine. I promise you. Also, I think it's a better idea if you stay away from anything that could be nefarious or the wrong side of the law, Rainer. None of us are losing you to jail again. And by the way, if I find out Brennan was responsible for your jail time, I'll take off his head.

"Not until we talk to him." Rainer smiled at his brother. "I've always felt that my brothers took that worse than I did."

Anton squeezed his arm. I had a house full of wolves, and it felt like we might finally be on the right side of this battle. Maybe.

ELEVEN

Hushed conversation filled the house as I tried to eat something before I tackled taking care of what had to be done next: fixing all the wolves who had been brought here from Miami.

"Don't choke on it." Rainer shot me a look as I chewed, and as fast as I could, swallowed the chicken he'd cooked.

Anton pulled my plate back.

"Hey..." I reached for it, and he shook his head. "What are you doing?"

I finished swallowing my chicken, and he broke off another piece of it before he offered it to me in his fingers. It took me a second to realize he wanted to feed me. He lifted an eyebrow in challenge. Was I going to fight him on that? No. I got what he was doing. He was pacing me.

I opened my mouth, and he put the chicken in. Jarret and Rainer watched the exchange, seemingly transfixed. Did they like that? Was feeding me... a thing?

I smiled at all of them as I chewed and swallowed. Was this a wolf thing, or just something these three liked? Anton gave me another bite.

Jarret sighed. "Wish I'd thought of that."

"Me, too." Rainer laughed.

Anton lifted his eyebrows as if to say that he wasn't at all sorry that he'd come up with it himself. Was it that his finger got to touch my mouth? "Seriously? What is sexy about this?"

I never got an answer, because Preston came in the room. "I'm out. I've got Isaac with me. A guy named Daniel and your father Drake, Mac. We're going to get Brennan. We'll find him, and he'll be made to answer for what he's done."

I ran toward him. "Be safe and come back to me. I can't lose you."

Preston's smile was all wolf. "I get to go hunting for you today. Do you know what an honor that is? I assure you, I will be back, in one piece, and with the first of those who harmed us. I've never felt stronger than I do right now. I've never been so sure that I'm on the right path. It is my privilege to bring you our enemy." He cupped my chin. "What I want more than anything are long lazy days, to come home from work to have you here telling me about your day. Someday, when things are safe and you're ready, to have babies with you." Warmth at his words flooded me. I let myself daydream, to go where his words took me. Those were beautiful images.

He continued. "I want lemonade and iced tea on the porch. This place filled with furniture you picked out, that you have an attachment to. So that you can say things like, hey, remember when we bought the couch, and they couldn't deliver it all the way out here so you had to haul it in the truck? Beer. Fancier drinks. Laughter. Slammed doors if we piss you off. I want to watch you take down your first alligator as a wolf. I want to be there to keep the wolves in order when they come to the Omega for help." He kissed both my cheeks. "I'm not going to die, because, so help me, I'm coming home and somehow, someway we're going to have that. All of it, and the things I can't think of yet.

I kissed his cheek. My voice broke when I said, "Thank you for all of that. Still, be careful. I have my own dreams, too. They all include you."

"Will do." He patted my ass on his way out the door. Worry made my stomach clench. I wasn't going to eat anything else tonight.

I watched him go, aware he took part of my heart with him. I hadn't had them back long enough to be sending them off, but circumstances made things impossible. I leaned against the table. "Hey, Anton, has anyone told you yet that you are the reason we found everyone? Thanks to your books."

He scrunched up his face. I guessed not. Rainer leaned next to me but made eye contact with his youngest brother. "It makes sense. The psychic link you talked about. Maybe he heard things or maybe he *heard* things. This is a whole side to being a wolf I never understood."

Anton ran past me, and I would have placed money that he was going to get copies of his books. I followed him but not to go to his books, rather to the living room where everyone waited.

Jarret leaned his chin on my shoulder. "What taxes you the least? One at a time or all at once?"

They all pretty much sucked equally. "I'm going to do it all at once, and then," I looked at Miranda, "I need to talk to you."

"And me." My mother rose. "If there are conversations to be had, I'm in on them."

"Me, too," Aurora added. I stared at both of those

women. Really? They wanted in on those conversations? My mother had never planned any wolf agendas in her life, and Aurora avoided it. But okay, maybe it was an in-law competitive thing. Sure. Why not?

Jarret kissed my cheek. "I'm going to go get you some water."

"Thanks." I squeezed his arm.

It was time to put an end to all of this. I looked down at my hands. When had I stopped noticing that they burned? Was it just such a constant in my life that I accepted it as normal? It was funny, really, I had no outward indication that my hands hurt.

They weren't red, or even particularly dry looking. If I touched them, they'd feel soft. There would be no discernible difference between my hands and the rest of me, and yet... they burned.

It felt better when I shifted, so I was going to do that before I took on this problem. I was a wolf shifter. These things I could do were actually meant to happen on all fours.

I called the shift onto myself and viewed the room more remotely. Some of the people were enemies. I could smell that metallic stink that meant they'd been infected with the wrongness. But they could end up smelling like pack. The rest of the people there did—every last one of them—because I'd fixed them, and that made them partially mine.

Lifting my head, I took another sniff. I'd marked even those who belonged to Miranda. They'd always have my scent. Why hadn't I realized that before?

I let my power loose. The room seemed to vibrate with it as I sent healing through my pores to them. It wasn't the burn I expected. Maybe my fur made the difference. Or maybe I was just stronger this way. It didn't really matter.

Around me the people in the room swayed, some of them shifting before they hit the ground, but all of them passing out. I watched it happen, a groan sounding in my throat. Even in my wolf state, I wasn't able to do this without taxing myself to the brink.

I stumbled and would have fallen, but another wolf nudged me. Rainer. He rubbed his body against mine. Had he shifted so he wouldn't pass out, or had he developed some kind of immunity to my ability so he didn't? Jarret ran over and knocked against me.

My heart surged. These were two of my mates. They were here. We were home. We were gaining pack. Now if only we could feast on the blood of our enemies, all would be well. I pulled myself up and stumbled again.

Rainer growled at the back of his throat. He wasn't happy with me stumbling around. Leaning on me, he forced me down to the ground until I settled. Jarret rubbed up against me, forcing me to stay still as Rainer did the same thing.

Anton walked out of the study, carrying one of his books in his hand. Well, that answered my question about whether or not my mates had resisted passing out because they'd been in wolf form. Anton still strode on two legs.

He knelt down and stroked my head before nodding at his brothers. His hand was gentle on me. Anton looked around the room, and then eyed me with a smile. Did he think it was amusing that I'd single handedly knocked everyone out all at once?

I pushed at Jarret and Rainer, who both finally let me up. I didn't want to lie around anymore. Even if I kept face planting or something, I wasn't going to give up the chance to be shifted like this, to run like a wolf. I'd craved it for weeks.

On not so steady feet, I ran out the back door and headed down toward the swamp. I turned around for a split second to see my brothers both coming out onto the porch. They were both in their wolf state. I guessed they weren't knocked out by my powers either. Was it possible for certain packmates to develop an immunity to it, or did they just not need any cleansing?

Right then, I didn't care. What I wanted to do was run. My nose told me what I should have expected to happen— Anton shifted while Rainer and Jarret took off after me. I'd no sooner made it to my destination than they were all with me.

I looked back at them. We were meant to do this. I ran swiftly toward the trees, not caring how it looked, or if I ended up regretting this later. I wanted this freedom that only came from getting to be this side of myself.

I lost track of time, but as I tired, Rainer eventually charged in front of me, forcing me to slow and then stop. I appreciated that he hadn't done that until I'd really been about to fall over and not able to get back up.

Anton leaped over me, giving me a wolfy smile before he lounged down on the ground like he didn't have a care in the world. I hadn't thought about safety, about us getting caught out here, and Rainer didn't smell like he was scared. They all seemed rather calm.

He called his wolf away and appeared in all his naked glory in front of me. "Shift back."

I did as he said, and a second later, Jarret and Anton were nude with me as well.

It was strange to be so comfortable out in the open and totally naked. Anyone could come by on an airboat and see us like this. I just couldn't bring myself to care.

"You're not invincible." Jarret spoke first, and I turned

to look at him. "When you use your power in sudden bursts like that, it has to take something out of you. Even if you're in your wolf form to do it."

He wasn't wrong. "I'm the only living Omega. The truth is that even surrounded by you guys, wearing your marks, I'm not sure how long I'll make it. The best I can do is give everything I have all the time to save our people, so that when I'm gone, they're okay. Maybe there will be other Omegas born when we can eliminate this threat. Maybe it's like some kind of protective thing. If he can wipe out all the Omegas, then the... universe or whatever... Preston isn't here to give me his explanation on that... made sure that there weren't Omegas to be wiped out."

Anton shook his head and pointed at me.

"Yes, except for me. I'm some kind of fluke."

Rainer pulled me against him. "Not a fluke. Maybe you were the only one strong enough to save us. And you're not dying. Not till you're an old lady, and I've gone first. I'm not accepting any other eventuality."

I laughed. It was a funny image. "Rainer, you know better than most that we don't get to pick our futures, and that we have little to no control over them."

I smelled the human the second my mates did. I whirled around, suddenly aware of my nakedness in a way I hadn't been when it had just been us. As if on cue to my statement, something buzzed by my head. Jarret's eyes widened before he slammed me down onto the ground. I sniffed the air.

There was only one of them.

"I know what you people are." It was an old woman's voice that shouted at us. Rainer crouched down and nodded to Anton while she shouted. "And my family is gone, but I still know. You're not natural. You're all monsters, and you deserve to die."

A shot again. This one didn't go anywhere near us. Whoever this woman was doing the shooting, wasn't that great of a shot. That didn't mean she couldn't get lucky. She'd already come rather close to us, and that was probably just a lucky aim.

Anton indicated to the left and shifted, fast. There was a scream. She might have thought she knew who and what we were, but my guess was she'd just seen it for herself for the first time. I tilted my head. When I'd been pretending to be human, I would have feigned sympathy for her. She was old, frightened, and likely confused.

But she'd just fired at us with a shotgun. I waited for the next shot. There it was. I sniffed the air. Anton was fine, he wasn't hurt in any way. The scream abruptly stopped.

I looked at Jarret, and he nodded at me. It was done.

The sounds of Anton padding over to us returned. He stared up at me with his wolf eyes, and like he had done for me earlier, I patted his head. "Thank you."

He rubbed against my leg.

"It would be just our fucking luck to get through all of the shit we've been through and get taken out by some human with a gun."

He was right. That would be just my fucking luck. I turned toward him. "What do we do about the body? That spot near the other house?"

"No, I'm going to go put her in the swamp. Let the gators have at her." Jarret walked toward where Anton had killed her. We didn't even know her name.

I looked at Rainer. "Should I be worried that I have so little care about the fact that we just ended a human life?"

"No. She took shots at you. That made her an enemy. We kill those who would harm us." He put his arm around me. "Let's go figure out what to do next."

I supposed it was better to acknowledge I wasn't human, and would not pretend that I was. In some ways, my wolf would always win the battle for my soul. It was simple, if someone didn't threaten us, they'd never have anything to fear from my pack. If they came at us, they weren't leaving alive.

WHAT IT TURNED out I needed to do was to help Rainer get everyone fed. As they woke up, the new people were as confused as everyone else. I was pretty sure that my brother's mating group had found two more mates. I didn't know for sure, because I had no time to ask him anything. Instead, I helped cook bacon and comforted people as they realized they'd lost months, sometimes years of their lives.

It didn't help that I was certain there were still wolves out there who needed our help. I'd no sooner handed someone a cup of coffee than the mothers—mine and my guys'—cornered me in the hall.

I looked between them. They were a formidable pair, both of them staring me down like they expected me to have the answers of the universe ready to hand over the second they asked for it.

"Sweetheart." My mother touched my arm. "What do you plan to do now?"

I swallowed. "Not sure, Mom. Preston is off doing something for us that might help move things along. As it is, I need to speak to Miranda, who is busy helping to calm everyone down, and see about figuring out where everyone should sleep, eat. The basics."

She nodded. "Well, all of that is important, but I mean what do you mean to do with this Omega thing."

"Omega thing?"

My mother-in-law rolled her eyes. "Omega thing? I wouldn't put it exactly like that. She is the Omega. That's all there is to it. And because she is, she has dragged my sons into the pit of danger where they are going to be under attack like this for the rest of their lives."

And there it all was. My mother didn't want me to be an Omega. She wanted me to stop it. My mother-in-law thought this was something I had done to her sons.

My temper had never been pretty and maybe it was less so now. But I had enough crap going on, and it was time to let these women, who would hopefully always be in my life, know how it was going to be.

"I'm the Omega. That is how it is. Period. I was born this way. I'm not sure if I picked it, or if I just am. I don't care. I can't fight against it. This is my role. I'm the only one who can do it, and so I shall. And as for your sons, they want to be here with me. I'd save them from this if I could. But they've made it very clear to me that they're in all the way. I believe them, because they're grown men, and they are capable of knowing their own hearts and brains. If it makes you feel better to think that I dragged them, then feel free to do so. I don't really care."

Anton was suddenly there. Maybe I hadn't heard him arrive because I was so focused on the fact that in the midst of this craziness, I still had to defend myself.

My youngest mate took my hand in his, drawing me to him. He stared at the women who'd raised us, and they both lowered their eyes. I looked up at him. He couldn't speak a word aloud, but he'd certainly made himself understood.

He leaned over and kissed my cheek, and then drew me away. I leaned on him, exceptionally tired.

Jarret rounded the corner. "What's going on? Something's wrong. I know it."

Anton looked over his shoulder, and Jarret followed where he indicated. He rolled his eyes.

"Mom. Oh, and Kenzie's mom. Great. Let me guess? They have some kind of issue. Are you taking her upstairs?"

Anton nodded, and Jarret looked past us. "I'm going to go remind mom she's supposed to be planning a funeral. I think she's in denial about it. Batter Kenzie rather than get to the unpleasant job of facing Kevin's death. Or maybe I'm just being kind. I'll handle your mother, too, Kenzie."

"You don't have to." I squeezed his hand. "Seriously, you don't have to make everything better. That's not your job. I was just really mean to them."

Anton shook his head, and Jarret laughed. "Seems like maybe you weren't so bad. Give me a minute. I want them to understand we're all on the same page."

"I think my mother thinks I can simply stop being the Omega. Like I might wake up and decide to set it aside."

Jarret cupped my cheek. "She's overwhelmed. You were taken, and she woke up, and you're pretty much the most important wolf born in a generation. Give it some time."

Anton rolled his eyes, and Jarret paused before he spoke again. "All right, maybe I'm being too kind. I'll be up in a minute."

I let Anton lead me upstairs. I'd cleared the entire house of pain. I wasn't as alone as I'd been without my mates, but I could still feel the empty. It hadn't gone away, it was just squished down where it was harder for it to reach me.

As I listened to the words said to me by two women who should have our best interests at heart but obviously didn't, the empty flared up, pushing at my center like it had every right to do so.

We were in Preston's room. It was the one with the most furniture at the moment, since he'd been living in the house before any of the rest of us had. Anton stopped me from moving farther in the room toward the bed.

"What?" Hadn't he brought me up here to rest? Even if he wanted sex, and I wouldn't say no to that if he did, it was going to happen on the bed.

He placed his hand right on my stomach, staring at me. Funny, that was just where I pictured the empty to be. He lifted his eyes to mine, and then dropped his gaze again.

"Can you feel that?" I could barely speak. "There is something inside of me, something that I think of as the empty. There was a time that it was all I had. It's smaller but it's there."

I wished I could read his thoughts, but when he shielded them I couldn't. Maybe there would be a time when he wouldn't have any reason to conceal them from me.

"It scares me when I can't immediately know what you're thinking. I know that's not fair. We're all entitled to our thoughts. I just..."

He kissed me, a sweet peck that joined our lips for a long moment. He smelled like home, like calmness. He wasn't turning to run. He didn't seem to be thinking that my describing the feelings that were inside of me as though they were real, intense entities that somehow existed separately from me was nuts. In fact, he'd known right where to touch to find it.

Anton let go of my mouth to kiss both my cheeks and squeezed his hand over the spot where I felt the empty. He tilted his head slightly, and I could read him just fine. Whatever it was that had been born of the pain, of the loneliness, of the terror, of the separation, it wouldn't be allowed to have me. It couldn't. Not when I already belonged to him and his brothers.

Jarret walked in the room and shut the door behind him. He looked at us for a second before he climbed on the bed. He patted the spot next to him. Anton followed me over, and I climbed in. He grabbed the blanket as he got in on the other side of me.

I was tired of being tired. I needed a day, maybe two, when I didn't have to use—as my mother put it—the Omega thing. I needed time to recharge. I would get none of that. Jarret pressed his hand to the waist of the sweatpants Rainer had given me. I had no underwear on, just the cotton athletic clothes that were slightly too big on me.

Anton kissed the back of my neck. They were intimate, kind touches from both of them that could have led to sex, but I knew it wasn't going to. Neither one of them had that heady scent that told me they wanted it to go there. No, this was just what love felt like. They recognized that I needed their touches, and maybe they needed mine, too.

"Sleep," Jarret whispered in my ear. "Your tiredness, the ache inside of you, is palpable like it's a presence in the room with us."

My empty. He'd just described it perfectly. I closed my eyes.

TWELVE

I woke myself up snoring. It was a strange feeling. I must have been really asleep. It had still been light outside when I fell asleep, and now it was dark. I rubbed at my eyes, and Jarret winced in sleep like my moving had bothered him. On my other side, Anton moved his head left and then right on the pillow. I studied them for a second, the light in the room from underneath the door not telling me nearly as much as their scents did.

They were both having bad dreams.

Rainer regarded me from the chair. Only his smell told me he was there, he would otherwise be lost in the darkness. I waved at him, and he rose, approaching the bed. "They've not been sleeping well. I wondered if it would wake you."

I lifted my hands, rubbing my fingers over their arms and then over their backs. My power reached out to them. Jarret made a sound in his throat before he soothed on a sigh. Anton's face relaxed, and the arm over me was suddenly less tense and more like dead weight.

I smiled at Rainer. "They're better now."

"Only because you're magic." He scooted Jarret over,

who flopped on his side, making a space for himself next to me. "I'll apologize to him in the morning."

I shook my head. "He'd do the same to you."

"I know it." He smiled at me. "Did you wake yourself up because you were snoring?"

I pinched him, and he grinned even wider. "I did, actually. Do I snore regularly?"

"Not before everything got fucked up. Now, I think it's utter exhaustion. You use so much power all the time."

I lifted an eyebrow. "So that would be, yes, I snore all the time."

He kissed my nose. "Yes. But none of us mind. Or at least I don't. Just tells me you're resting. I saw how you were when I got back. I'd rather have you snoring than like that. Besides, Preston snores like he's sawing something. You're much daintier."

"Dainty snoring." I rolled my eyes. I was wide-awake now. "Is everyone out cold?"

"Yep, even Miranda, who said to tell you that as soon as you've had coffee in the morning that you're hers for a long stretch."

That made sense. We'd had our wires crossed so far, but we needed to have a long talk.

"You're not tired." He smoothed my hair. "It's like you had a nap. It's going to be hard for you to sleep now."

I nodded. "A million rapid thoughts. That's what I'm focused on. Like is Preston okay? Where is everyone going to sleep? Are there more humans with shotguns?"

He linked our fingers. "Yes, he texted. He has a lead on Brennan. Thinks he'll be able to grab him first thing tomorrow. Everyone is spread out among the two houses. We may take one of the abandoned mansions and start repurposing it. It has no working plumbing, but maybe that's a task we could give someone. There are always humans with shotguns."

With our fingers linked, I could actually feel his exhaustion. I let go of his hand to run my fingers down the exposed skin on his arm.

He moaned. "Your powers are on. You don't have to do that. I'm okay."

"Ssshh. I'm soothing you. Then when you fall asleep, I can listen to you breathe and tell you whether you snored or not."

He laughed. "There was a big empty hole in my heart, and it needed you to fill it."

His words kind of slurred together. It had to be my power, and I kept stroking my hand over his exposed skin. He made the sigh sound again, this time deeper. "Seriously, MacKenzie, you don't have to do that."

"Stop arguing and enjoy it." What did it feel like to have someone do this? To have an Omega soothe bad feelings?

Rainer shifted slightly. "If you knock me out like this, my love, it's going to make me dream about you. I'm going to wake up hard as a rock."

I leaned on my elbow. "That would be bad, why?"

"Not bad." He shook his head. "Just saying. Do you want to have a baby?"

Now that took me by surprise. "Not at this very moment, no."

"That makes sense. I don't want one currently, either. But I do want one with you. A lot of them. A big, wolf family like there used to be. Do you think they'll mind I went to jail?"

I tilted my head. Rainer was out of it. He might as well have been asleep. "The children? No, they won't mind. They'll never think about it, and if they do, it won't be in a negative way. We can always explain. I think it bothers you more than it will ever bother anyone else. Particularly because you didn't do anything. They scapegoated you to get to your family."

"Hmmm." He moved his head slightly. "And they took away the restaurant I was going to have someday."

I leaned over and kissed his chin. "We'll get that back, too."

"I... Fuck, I don't know what I'm saying. It's like you put a warm bath in my mind. I'm floating."

"Then close your eyes and float off to sleep. You have more than earned it. I'll stay right here. You don't have to worry."

"I'm sorry we had a fight. Let's never have one again."

Well, I doubted that would be possible. We were probably going to have another fight at some point. "We can try."

"You know what?"

I didn't let him finish that. I placed my fingers gently on his eyes and closed them. He didn't make a sound as he drifted away. I'd never seen Rainer drunk, but I'd bet it was like that. That had to be on the list of things to do. Get drunk with my mates. Stupid, happy, laughing, passed out intoxicated.

Babies? He'd brought up babies. Was that even something we could think about? Preston had said that, too. Was I allowed to daydream about a someday where I could be a mother? Or did I have to imagine that my life as the only Omega meant there would never be time for me?

"Kenzie?" Jarret spoke, but I could tell from his scent he was asleep.

I reached across Rainer and rubbed his arm. "I'm fine."

I lay in the darkness until once again, I found sleep.

I stared at the older woman looking back at me. "He'll bring the fight to you."

I nodded. "We're ready for that. He isn't going to be able to zap their ears and take their minds like they did before. I've cleaned them."

She walked away from me, and I followed after her. The sun was setting, and the sand was warm but not too hot on my feet. I stared down, and then up again. We were on a beach. How had we gotten on a beach?

"I'm not talking about that. You've taken away that option. You're fixing the shifters. Packs will start reforming. Frankly, I'm not sure how you're even doing that. It would have killed me. He killed me."

I stared at her for a second. "You're an Omega."

She snapped her fingers in front of my face. "Wake up. Wait, not literally. Yes, I am an Omega. You're dreaming."

I sighed. That was disappointing, just about as awful as I could fathom. "I'm asleep. Back in Louisiana, wrapped up against Anton and Rainer with Jarret close by. I've made you up."

She waved her hand. "Not really. I mean, no, I'm not real. I'm dead. That doesn't mean I'm not here with you."

That didn't make the slightest bit of sense. But I supposed that dreams never did. I shook my head. "Well, maybe I'll meet you in person if there is some kind of after-life, because this whole thing is going to kill me."

She nodded. "It sure might."

Even my dreams couldn't be pleasant. That was so typical of me.

"He was able to kill all the Omegas, and no more were born. Until you." The old woman tilted her head, her long white hair glistening in the sunset like it had sparkles sewn into it. "The question really is, how did you get here at all?"

I blinked. "That's the question? Not... what is he? Not... how did he do all this stuff? How am I here? That's what you want to talk about?"

She winked at me. "I've never met another Omega I liked. Until you."

I woke up. The sun bathed the room in kind rays. It was early. Jarret lifted his head and looked at me from across Rainer. "How did I lose my spot?"

Rainer smiled, his eyes still closed. "Snooze you lose, brother."

Jarret growled in the back of his throat. "Oh, it's on now, Rainer. You wait. You're going to wake up on the floor next time."

I giggled, and Anton kissed my neck, bringing my attention to him. It was almost perfect right then, but Preston was missing, and that was a big giant hole. "I have to go find Miranda."

Rainer kissed my cheek. He still hadn't opened his eyes. "So what you're saying is, that we can't just let everyone rot."

I smiled. "Unfortunately, not. The whole Omega thing." Saying that brought to mind my dream from the night before. "Hey, weird thing..."

A knock sounded on the door, and I sat up, pulling the sheet over all of us. Rainer finally lifted his head. He took a long breath. "It's Miranda. Guess she's tired of waiting."

I couldn't blame her. "Great nose you have there. All I can scent is an overabundance of wolf in the house. Like it's all just becoming one giant smell."

He kissed my arm. "Go."

Anton let go of me, and I scooted out of the bed. "Coming, Miranda."

"Great." She laughed. "I'm not leaving the hallway in

case something happens that gets in your way of talking to me."

I smiled. I couldn't blame her for her caution. Things did seem to happen that screwed up my best laid plans.

"SO THAT IS IT. That is what happened." I drank my coffee and regarded Miranda across the dock. We were alone outside. People came and went inside the house. As far as I could tell, Rainer was in his element, cooking for large amounts of people, Jarret had taken off to one of the nearby mansions to show it to some other shifters, and Anton had locked himself in his study to write.

People were giving Miranda and me a wide berth.

She shook her head. "He's... he's connecting and controlling through the psychic link that connects all wolves. I'll be damned. Somehow, he used that to kill the Omegas, and now he's after you. Got through your mate shields. This is serious."

I nodded. "Yes, I know. Have you heard anything about this, ever?"

She rubbed her face. "Nothing even close to this."

Well, there went that. "I was thinking," I sighed, "what happens to Loups if we don't clear them? What happens over time?"

"Well you've seen them, a lot of them from what I gather. You're getting to be quite a legend, actually."

I wasn't the least bit interested in rumors or anything like that. "What happens to them if we never get to them?"

She blinked. "I... I don't know. We don't see them again when they really vanish. Like they reach a point where we stop spotting them. They're just in the wind."

They didn't just disappear. I rubbed my eyes. Where was my dream Omega now to answer some questions? The woman, if she had ever been real to begin with, was now dead. She hadn't survived this mess. And if she wasn't real, then she was a figment of my imagination who had no idea anyway, since I didn't know. I wanted to puke. What did it mean that I preferred the second option to the first? I couldn't be communicating with the dead.

Unless somehow it was inherited knowledge. Like the way sometimes animals shared information, genetically imparted from one generation to the next. Was this how that happened for me?

I had to get back to the subject at hand. The Loup Garous. They went mad. Usually lone wolves, but since we eliminated packs, it happened in larger amounts. And females weren't immune to it. They didn't become the walking-on-two-legs-while-they-shifted monsters, but they suffered through madness.

Did it just get worse?

I paced to the end of the dock. The swamp stared back at me. I jolted at the thought. That was ridiculous. The swamp wasn't staring at me. While living things existed in the swamp, the area itself wasn't alive. It didn't look at anything.

I tilted my head and continued to stare. Taking a deep breath, I searched for clarity. Why was I hyper focusing on the swamp, when I should be thinking about the Loups? I chewed on my lip. Maybe because they were created.

A log slowly floated past. Was it a log, or was it a gator? I wasn't all that good at telling. For all that I craved this place, I hadn't spent enough time here to really learn it. I breathed deeply. It was a gator. My eyes turned wolf, and I smiled. In other circumstances, could I kill that gator? I longed to try, but resisted the urge.

I turned my head. Someone not being careful might think that creature was a log. And they might end up as the alligator's lunch. Things weren't exactly what they seemed.

Like the Loups weren't always what they seemed.

"Miranda." I spoke to her without turning around. "There can't be Loups running around uncaught. We are nothing if not careful as beings. We are designed to hide from the fucking humans."

She stepped next to me. "Is that an alligator?"

I nodded. "It is."

Miranda rubbed her arms. "They hide pretty well, too. In plain sight. I thought that was..."

"A log," I finished for her. "Like I might think that a Loup was just a human. The more we tried to become like the humans, the more Loups there were. But there were no Loups caught, no humans figured us out."

Because the more we became like them, the more the madness on the outside became hidden away, trapped and only evident in our minds. That's why Ross had seemed so off to me, yet familiar. He was a Loup. A very old one, a very powerful presence. And he had us all by the proverbial balls.

"Did anyone used to keep track of Loups? Like would you have a record of one named Ross Morgan. Whose pack he was in, how long ago that would have been?"

She shook her head. "We don't keep records. Humans can find those."

I knew that better than most. If any Omegas had decided to keep records, I might know better what I was doing.

"I don't suppose it matters anyway. He's a Loup. I fix Loups. It's what I do."

She tilted her head. "He's very dangerous. I mean... if the Loup madness is only visible in his mind, then he's out there doing all of this in the daylight. He doesn't have to hide at all. We know he's employed humans. He has a whole network of support. I don't think this is going to be a question of you just walking up to him and doing what you do. I think you should expect a bigger battle. Even if it's just the two of you in a room."

I shivered, even though there was no chill in the air, just in the words that she spoke.

Anton strode toward us, and Miranda looked at me. "You know, I wondered if you guys ever had trouble communicating. But even I can smell his intent right now. He has something on his mind."

I smiled. I didn't need my heightened sense of smell to know that. The slope of his brow would have alerted me, and fortunately, my inability to gather his thoughts had passed. We were back on the same page.

When I smelled Anton's approach, all I could scent was his love for me. Fuck. I was such a lucky woman.

He nodded at Miranda, and she acknowledged him the same way. "I have to think about some of this, MacKenzie. If you're right, then we have to reevaluate everything we think we know about Loups. This could be a huge crisis."

We were already in a crisis, but I didn't need to point that out right now. She knew it as well as I did. Anton held up one of his books. He'd stuck his finger in one page like a bookmark, keeping it open that way.

I took it from him, making sure to keep it open to where he'd marked. "You found something?"

He nodded and pointed. I looked down at the page.

He'd circled an entire paragraph. It had to do with a character taken with madness. He was trying to kill all the aliens. I bit my lip and read. After a second, I looked up at him. "This goes in line with everything I've been thinking."

Anton nodded fast. He pulled a sheet of paper out of his pocket. I took it from him, reading what he'd written.

I always felt weird about the whole passage. Like I wrote it, but not like the others. Like those details you used to find us. It felt like that.

That made sense. He'd been connected to these people for years. There might be a million details like this. "Thanks for thinking of it. Just confirms what I was saying. I need to find Ross. I can put a stop to this whole thing."

He grabbed my arm, and I stared at him for a second before he shook his head. My heart clenched. Anton didn't want me anywhere near Ross. I cupped the side of his cheek. "Believe me, I have no death wish. No interest whatsoever in being some kind of werewolf martyr. But if I'm the only one on the planet who can make this stop, then I'll do that."

My youngest mate looked up at the sky, and then back at me. His frustration rolled off him in droves. We needed to find his tablet. His eyes turned wolf, and for a second, he let me see all of his hostility, the need to kill, and I knew he didn't want to hurt me, those sensations weren't directed at me. They were for Ross.

His fangs descended. If Anton wasn't careful, he was going to turn this half shift into a full one. I ran my finger over the edge of one of them. They were sharp. "You could kill him. That's what you're saying. You could shift, and you could tear him into pieces."

He nodded, the fangs going back up, and his eyes returning. "I know you could kill him, and will if you get the chance. The problem? I'm not sure it's that simple. He can't have made it this long if it were just a matter of wolfing out on him and taking care of business. He systematically took you and some of the others down to bring down the pack system, and leave us vulnerable to creating more Loups. What we're talking about is pretty out there."

I kissed his cheek just to breathe him in. When I spoke again, it was a whisper in his ear. "I don't want him anywhere near any of the people I love again. Not you. Not Jarret. Not Preston. Not Rainer. Not any of our families. Kevin is dead. And countless others. I'm not... I'm going to kill him, and that'll be the end of it."

He lifted his eyebrows. His skepticism rolled off him in waves.

The sound of cars caught my attention from around the other side of the house. I sniffed the air and a second later, Preston's scent caught my attention. Anton and I grinned at the same time. Preston was back.

He grabbed my hand, and we rushed around the side of the house together. His joy at Preston's arrival filled me with utter happiness. They hadn't been like this when I'd first met them. The house had been so filled with mistrust and anger, that I'd never have imagined such a turn around. My mates needed pack like they required air.

How had Anton gone so many years without Preston? How had Jarret gone without Rainer? And why had the universe been smiling at us the day they'd all been together for my arrival?

Was it fated, or like Preston thought, that just in split seconds our wolves decided they liked each other and had what we each needed? Did it matter? We were family. They'd let me into their lives and centered themselves around me like it was the most natural thing to do.

Preston strode toward us. "I got him. Tied up in the trunk."

That was great, but I was more excited to see him, than whatever would happen next. I wrapped my arms around him, drawing him close. I kissed him. He smiled against my mouth as heat flooded me. "You missed me."

I was off my feet while he spun me around. "I missed you, too."

"Don't drop my sister," Isaac said as he walked past us. "We all helped. But Preston took him down. Almost like a man possessed. It was impressive."

Preston set me down and nodded at my brother before he embraced his own. "You doing okay, kid?"

Anton rolled his eyes, but it was with nothing but affection.

"Good job not dying," Rainer called from the porch. Jarret wasn't home, but I was sure when he got back there would be an excited greeting from him, too. We were meant to spend our life together.

Preston nodded at Rainer. "Thanks. Want me to leave this asshole in the trunk for a while?"

Rainer shook his head. "You've had all the fun. I'll get him out. I don't want an audience for this. So, let's take him to one of the empty houses. Much as I appreciate you wanting to hold our mate, go shift and use your nose to find Jarret. Get him to the house all the way on the end. It's probably a knock down and perfect for our needs."

Preston let go of me. "On it." He winked at me. "I promised you I would defeat our enemy. For you."

His eyes were all wolf, and mine turned in response. "You did as you promised."

He kissed me hard. Then, he let go. Shifting mid-stride,

he took off running. Anton's eyes had turned too as he stared at Rainer.

"Help me out, little brother. We are going to make this man pay for whatever role he played in this."

I put my hands on my hips. "You know, he might be under mind control. Like you all were. He could be sick. Every one of you would have hurt me if you could. He might have been following orders."

"Maybe." Rainer strode past me. "But I don't think so. Brennan strikes me as a guy who puts his own interests over everyone else's. If I'm wrong, I'll apologize for banging him around. If I'm not, he's going to wish he'd never been born."

THIRTEEN

Rainer dragged Brennan from the trunk of the car. The other man fought but didn't attempt to shift. Anton's eyes were wolf as he followed after them. My guess would be if Brennan made any moves to become a wolf, Anton would beat him to it and take him down before he could.

I watched them for a moment before I followed them. My oldest mate was making it hurt. My mouth watered with anticipation. I was bloodthirsty. It was in my nature, and right now, I didn't feel like doing a single thing to stop it. Why bother? We lived in a bloody time, and we had to be animal enough to embrace it before we ended up dead ourselves.

With those thoughts prompting me, I took off after them. The sounds of the swamp were all around me, and like before, I was struck by how quickly the place could go from quiet to deadly. Sort of like me. I looked human, but I wasn't. This place wasn't safe. It was hidden from the world and perfect for us to keep our secrets.

Why had we ever left this oasis and gone to Colorado? Why hadn't my parents liked it here? And where were the rest of my family? These were questions that drove me forward.

I rounded the corner as Preston and Jarret showed up from the other side. Jarret kissed my cheek before he ran into the house, but Preston stopped. With a wink, Preston grabbed me, picking me up again like he'd done earlier. "Hey, if you want to greet me like you did when I got home every day when I get back from work, I'd fucking love it. Rush out to the car. It was the best thing I've ever seen."

I shook my head at him. "You'd get tired of it."

"There's nothing about you I could get tired of."

I kissed both his cheeks. "You're so good to me. Is your business okay?"

"I have no idea. I'm truly forcing myself to not find out. I can't go to work right now. So, I can't do anything about it. Maybe the whole thing will implode. I guess I'll find out later." He shrugged. "Ready to do this thing?"

A scream burst out into the air around us, and we both turned to stare, our eyes flipping to our wolf sides immediately. Preston, dressed in throwaway clothes we left around, took a deep breath. "Smells like Rainer got started without us."

I nodded. "Where did you snatch Brennan from?"

"His bed. He was hiding in a cheap motel, but it wasn't hard to find him. I pulled him from his bed. If he wasn't actively resisting his wolf, it would have been harder."

I squeezed his arm. "Let's get this over with."

The house Rainer had dragged Brennan to was empty and falling apart. Jarret stared down at the man while Rainer kneeled in front of him.

"Sorry about the yelling," Rainer said, not looking at us. He nodded toward Anton who stood by the window. "Anton kicked him pretty hard."

I couldn't say I was sorry about that. Without looking up again, Rainer spoke. "Does he need to be healed, my love?"

That was a good question. "I don't know if my hands are burning because he was injured from the kick, or because he's been under Ross' control. I think we'd better determine which before we proceed any further."

My oldest mate nodded. "Okay. He killed our father, so you'll have to excuse us if we have no sense of reason at the moment. Kevin was one of the best people I've ever known. And now he's gone. In his place will be a big gaping hole that my mother will never heal from, and that the rest of us will have to learn how to live with. She, by contrast, will feel that ache in a way that can never be settled every day she draws air."

Brennan lifted his head. "I didn't want to do that, but to keep everyone alive, I have to do what the corporations tell me to do."

I squatted down next to Rainer. "We already know that's a lie. It's not corporations. It's one man. His name is Ross. Our question isn't are we right, we know we are, our question is do you know?"

Recognition flooded his gaze, and I stepped back. Yes, the man was in pain, but no, he wasn't being mind-controlled, but rather following a power-hungry Loup with the money and time to try to destroy us all. Brennan knew exactly what he was doing.

Maybe he'd even concocted the corporation story.

I rose. "He's not being controlled by Ross."

Rainer lifted his gaze to meet my own. "Got it."

Perhaps Omegas in the past had been altruistic. Maybe they were forgiving. But it wasn't my job to save this man from his wolf destiny. Screw with a pack, and you faced the

Alpha. I'd only been an active werewolf for a short period of time, and even I understood that. Most of Brennan's life had been spent before the Accords he'd thrust on all of us came into existence.

Before I left, I just had one question. "Why?"

"Why?" He managed to pull himself up on his knees but only because Rainer allowed it. "You haven't been in his presence. He's a god, MacKenzie. A werewolf god. What he says goes. Period. He wants werewolves gone. I did what I could for us. The Accords really were to save us. If we didn't act like werewolves, he left us alone. On occasion, he'd take one or two werewolves from wherever and do something to them." His gaze flew to Anton. Oh yes, we knew just what it was that he did to werewolves he took.

He'd never say a word aloud because of them, and he had been the catalyst for all of the people in our group who went under Ross' control.

I touched the side of Brennan's face. Not to heal him, but just so I could be sure he'd listen to the words I said. "I understand you completely. You're a coward. A big fat scaredy wolf, and you have done damage to everyone thanks to your cowardice. You're going to live long enough to feel a lot of pain, and then not much longer after that. But make no mistake, you will suffer."

"Stop."

We all turned to look at the same time. My mother-in-law, Aurora, stood in the doorway. Gus and Cristian were behind her. I sniffed the air. I was losing my touch if I hadn't noticed them coming. Well, I could scent them just fine now. It had all been a lot to take in lately.

"That's Brennan." She strolled into the room, her chin high, her back straight. Dark circles marred her peach complexion. Anger. Hate. Those were scents I could read just fine. It was like I was losing the ability to tell that individuals were around, but their emotions still rode me hard.

"He's why Kevin died." Her voice choked, and tears hit my eyes. Aurora didn't need me to clear her. She was mourning one of her loves. There wasn't going to be any making that any better. She'd already lost one husband.

I turned to stare at my mates. I'd lost them once, but Kevin wasn't coming back from where he'd gone. I pushed away my tears. Those were human emotions, and I was partly that, but we were werewolves. Fuck crying. What we all needed was blood.

"Let your mother kill him."

Gus nodded at me like I'd said exactly the right thing. I glanced at Rainer. He'd been ready to take care of Brennan. His eyes were pure wolf, and rage wafted off him in waves the likes of which I had never smelled on him before.

He stepped back. "Mom?"

My mother-in-law shifted. I'd never seen her as a wolf before. Or maybe I had when I'd fixed her. I didn't remember. They were all becoming sort of a blur to me. One fix after another. I was happy to do it, but I couldn't decipher them anymore, not like I had with those first Loups.

Mid-stride she became a wolf. One second she was lovely, ethereal, and the next she was covered in dark gray fur. I lifted my lids wider and watched as she launched herself at Brennan.

Anton tugged on the end of my hair, drawing me close to him. I loved that. We were going to watch this together. Brennan tried to shift, but it was slow, hard looking. Maybe he could have used some healing to help with that.

I didn't care.

Perhaps the Omegas of old were all forgiving. I would

never be that. His pain was justified. It tasted right in my mouth.

Anton pressed his nose against my shoulder, and Jarret walked over.

Their mother tore at Brennan's skin, and we watched it like we observed a movie, or maybe more like a boxing match.

Rainer jumped backward, getting out of his mother's way. Blood splattered on his shirt, but it didn't look like he noticed or cared. He smiled at the scene. Yes, that man who now screamed at the top of his lungs had killed his sire. We usually didn't know in our families which of our fathers were our biological one. It didn't matter. I loved all of mine the same, and they never treated me as anything but their own. Yet, there hadn't been a question that Rainer was Kevin's. He looked just like him. Alpha personality to Alpha personality. Kevin had been the glue to their family in a lot of ways.

This man had been responsible for what happened to Anton. I turned to him. "Do you want a turn?"

He shook his head, not picking his nose up from where it pressed in my shoulder. His arms wrapped around me. All right, this was his mother's kill.

Brutal. Bloody. Noisy.

Perfect.

If I'd had any question that I could go back to ever pretending to be fully human again, it fled. I wasn't human. I was a werewolf. And when we took down our enemies, we did it in blood.

We hadn't asked him where Ross was. We'd gotten no other information than Brennan's responsibility in what occurred. The rest we would work out. Maybe I'd regret not spending more time, later. But this was our way. And justice was ours.

THE SOUND of music greeted us as we approached the house. It was upbeat, Cajun sounding. Someone with a low, scratchy voice sang about New Orleans and the heart. I smiled. It did feel like we should have a party.

But then again, that might be highly inappropriate. I wasn't at all sure about my reactions right now.

"Hey." I squeezed Anton's hand. Gus had taken their mother off with Cristian. I didn't know where, and I didn't ask. Some things were better left private.

He raised his eyebrows, which prompted me to continue. "How did you know that part of the book you found was about Ross?"

Anton squeezed my hand and pulled me along. Jarret ran to catch up to us. "That's a good question. I need details on this."

Preston yawned. "It took a lot of us a lot of time to figure them out the first time. Without your insight, Anton. Did you just know when you looked?"

He gave me an annoyed glance. There were some things that had to make him feel frustrated. I rubbed his arm. "Do we know where his tablet is?"

Jarret shook his head. "No, but I'll order another. Get it here fast. Those fuckers probably stole it when they came here and attacked us."

The sounds of a car screeching caught my attention, and I looked over my shoulder at our house. What the hell?

Rainer growled. "We have company."

In retrospect, we should have seen it coming. The only

excuse I could see for not knowing this was going to happen, was that we'd all embraced our wolves for only months. Somehow, we had to think like humans and werewolves at the same time. The more we embraced one over the other, the more we were in trouble.

It was endless. It was constant. It was our existence.

The humans—the ones employed by Brennan—were here. I recognized their scents immediately from the time they'd stolen my loves from me and killed my father-in-law.

Jarret shifted before I could even consider what was going to happen and charged at the car. The house emptied out. I didn't even know if everyone knew who these humans were, but they must have caught a scent of something they didn't like, because suddenly we were an army of werewolves.

Rainer's eyes shifted, then his hands. He looked at me, and I nodded. I knew what he wanted. I'd stay back. I took two steps and then a third to get out of the way. I wanted to fight. It took every ounce of my strength to stop myself from doing so.

The smell of the adrenaline, of the other wolves shifting into battle was almost too much. I wanted to join them. Craved it.

Anton met my gaze. He hadn't shifted, but Jarret had. I'd lost track of him, although I was certain I'd know if he or Preston or Rainer weren't okay. I'd always know. That was part of my gift. With my mates, I was that connected.

"You can go." I spoke through gritted teeth. "I'm staying right here."

He winked at me before he shifted into his wolf form. I leaned back against Gus' truck and watched. One of the humans, a big burly man, pulled out the device he'd used last time to control Anton that triggered the psychic response in the others. I jolted. I'd fixed them, and I could do it again, but this was how we'd know if I'd managed to do it permanently, or if we were on an endless loop. One that would never stop, where they were able to hurt us, and we couldn't really make headway.

I bit my lip, and I waited. Nothing happened except for the battle continuing. They hadn't been able to hurt us. I grinned, true elation flooding my system. I hadn't known I needed this moment, but I did.

Where was Miranda? I found her in the crowd. No wonder she was Alpha of her pack. The woman was strong. Two humans went down. How many more were there?

I started to count. They'd come out of cars and vans. That was stupid. Even the hunter in the swamp with a shotgun had been smarter than this. Ross didn't find the cream of the crop when it came to humans.

Rainer caught my eye. A human ran toward him, and he backed up, letting him pass. Why would he do that? The thought flew through my mind a second before I realized the answer. He was letting me have him. I grinned, calling the shift onto myself.

I sometimes wished I could just stay as a wolf. Life would be so much simpler. Everything made sense like this. I jumped onto the human and tore at his neck. The fact that Rainer had let me have this didn't dampen the thrill.

This was battle. This was pack. This was life.

I'd had my one kill, and now it was over. Anton banged into me, catching my attention. He smelled like mine. I knocked back into him, and he smiled.

This had been easy. I'd deal with the ramifications of that later. Ross hadn't survived however long he had by being stupid. He was a Loup, and that made him insane, but that didn't mean he wasn't smart. He'd already proven himself to be adept at finances since, somehow, he'd managed all of this.

If I didn't want to kill the madman, I'd actually be completely interested in his story. How had he gone from Loup lost in the world to mad genius? How long had he been like this? How old was he?

We might never know these things, since our priority had to be elimination and not giving the man an interview and a therapy session.

My body burned. We had injuries in this pack. I needed to heal people. I blinked. They really were all pack right now. That was new. They might not stay this way. Miranda would take her people and go home, that included my brother. But for now, they were all here, and they were all mine. Not because I was in charge of them. No, if anything, that would be Rainer, but because they were mine to care for.

I sniffed the air. There had been so much pain. There would be so much pain to come. But for now, things were beautiful.

I shifted back. Along with everyone else involved, I had to find clothes, and scurrying around to locate items to cover up with was less embarrassing than I might have imagined it would be. We were all naked. It was like communal discomfort we all quickly ignored and fixed. Maybe if we were all going to be here for a while, we should hide clothes in various places around the swamp. Was that possible, or would the animals tear through the bags?

I chewed on my lip and thought about it.

One second I was doing that, and the next, I faced Ross.

We were back again on the dock that wasn't real. It was just him and me.

Annoyance made my back stiff. I'd been afraid last time, this occurrence, not so much.

"Again?" I shook my head. "You must really like me."

He smiled and stepped toward me. "The opposite, actually. It annoys me to no end that you exist. I can't really fathom how. I've stopped the birth of an Omega for a generation. How did you get here?"

I swallowed. I had no answers for him. "How did you manage to do that?"

Question for a question often deflected things. Or at least, that's how my brother used to get out of trouble when he snuck out late at night.

He scowled at me. "Haven't you figured it out yet, Omega? It's all about our psychic connection. We smell the link through our noses, but it comes down to the fact that we inherently know which one of us is the strongest one around. I sent out the message to every werewolf that no Omegas were to be born, and none were. And yet... here you are."

That was true. "Maybe my parents aren't good listeners."

"Oh, it's not them." He sneered. "I've tested them. They're not strong. The problem is you."

I blinked. I needed to get control of this situation and fast. "Maybe you're not stronger than me. Maybe I'm stronger than you."

He smiled. "There was a time when I would have killed for an Omega to find me, to heal me. But none did. None did!" He shouted the last bit, and I flinched. "Are you stronger than me? Not yet. I can't let you spoil what I've worked so hard to make. Don't you understand, Omega? I am saving the world. No one will ever have to suffer as I have again. No one will ever have to know my pain."

I stepped toward him. "I'm sorry that no one found you. I truly am. Come to me. I'll help you."

"Omega, you just killed dozens of humans. You have big problems ahead of you. And you're not going to help me. I know it. You'd kill me, too."

I shook my head. "I wouldn't."

I wasn't even lying. No way would I be allowed to be the one to kill him. One of my mates would in a heartbeat. Maybe that was semantics, but I was stuck in a mind meld with a Loup. Who was going to judge me for playing word games?

"I can't have you out there clearing people. You've already set me back. All of those wolves have to be reacquired. I won't have it."

"They're mine now. Not yours. You can't have them."

"Yes, I can." He leaned forward. "The only thing I need to do is take out you."

In this... whatever this place was... he couldn't touch me. I'd figured that out last time. We were both here in our minds but not in our...

I cried out as pain flooded me. Sharp, electrical, horrifying pain. I fell backward.

"Stronger than me? No." He snarled, showing his wolf teeth for the first time. "Here's what you Omegas don't understand. We are meant to be Loups. We don't need you to fix us." That was a direct contradiction to what he'd just said, but Loups were always off, and I was in too much pain to care right then. I grabbed onto my head.

It was cloudy.

"You want to heal me? You can't. I'm not broken." He shouted. "But only the strong survive in this world. You won't be able to stop me. You won't be able to do a thing, Omega. You won't have mates. You have no future. This?

It's how I killed all the Omegas. You can't clear a Loup when you are one."

When I was... what?

I blinked, and I stood in the living room of our house. Music played and half-dressed shifters laughed around the room. I stared at them. Why was it so bright in here? I winced, looking up. Did we have to have every light on in the house? There was still sunlight outside. I mean... fuck.

"You okay?" Jarret stood next to me, tilting his head while he spoke. "Your scent. It just went... off."

I shrugged. "What do you want from me, Jarret? I don't control my scent."

He opened and closed his mouth. "Okay. That's true. Um, Kenzie? Nope. Something is wrong."

"Nothing is wrong except that it's too bright in here." Okay, I shouted. I did. Loud enough that everyone in the room turned to stare at me. Jarret didn't seem to care. With eyes only on me, he reached out and grabbed my arm.

I wrenched his back. His fingers burned. I rubbed at my skin. "Don't touch me."

Rainer strode across the room. "MacKenzie?" He said my name but looked at Jarret. "What's going on? Her scent. It's wrong."

"Doesn't want to be touched. Too bright. Really short-tempered. Not acting like herself."

What I needed was for all of them to leave me alone. Anton came out of the office and Preston down the stairs. Great. Now I was going to be inundated. "Can't a person have a headache?"

I turned on my heel and ran for the door. But Jarret was faster. He stared at me a long moment, blocking my way. "No."

A growl in my throat, I shoved at him. He had to move. I

didn't even manage to push him at all. Strong arms came around me from behind. Preston. I fought against him. Why couldn't they all just leave me alone?

"Something wrong?" Miranda asked Preston as he picked me up.

Anton nodded as an answer, and they all turned around at the same time. Rainer touched my cheek. "She's hot."

"I can feel her distress like its inside of me." Jarret ran a hand through his hair. "One second she stood there, the next this happened. Could something have gone wrong in the fight?"

"No, that happened before. One second one thing, then another second something else. The last time Ross grabbed her consciousness. We hadn't known then. Mac, did you see Ross?"

Why were they blathering on? I had to get out of here. My fangs burst through my gums. "Let me go, or I'll make you."

Miranda covered her mouth. "Just like my sister."

Why wasn't anyone listening to me?

FOURTEEN

Rainer locked us all in his bedroom. Things were strewn everywhere. He wasn't neat. The room was filled with scents I didn't recognize. Others had been sleeping in here. Their smells made me want to gag. I had to get away from here. I needed to be alone. In the swamp. I could *be* there.

Anton held up a tablet. I guessed he'd found it.

"She smells wrong. Like they do, the Loups." The low machine voice spoke for him.

Rainer sniffed the air. "You're right. Why didn't I notice it? Subtle but there."

I laughed, throwing my head back. "Because none of you can ever scent exactly what I do. Why should you have to bother when, gee, you can throw an Omega at the problem?"

Jarret winced. "I hate the sound of sarcasm in her voice. It's not Kenzie."

I pointed at all of them. "If any of you try to touch me, I will scratch out your eyes."

My oldest mate walked toward me, hands up like he was considering surrendering. That wasn't what his scent told me. Oh no, he was an Alpha wolf, and he was ready, willing, and able to subdue me. Well, I had news for him. I wasn't going to be stopped. I was getting out of here. The Swamp called to me. There were too many people in this house.

"You know somewhere deep inside of you that I would never hurt you." He looked over his shoulder at Jarret. "Neither would he." He nodded toward Anton. "Or him."

What was he doing?

Strong arms came around me from behind, stopping me from moving when I wanted to rear back. Preston. Damn it. How had he gotten the jump on me?

"Look." I wasn't above pleading. "I have to get out of here."

"I know that you think that," Preston said in my ear. "But you're not well." He ran his finger over the mark he'd given me and something inside of me stirred. That felt so nice, so familiar, so home.

Tears came to my eyes. "Something's wrong with me."

Rainer nodded at Preston. "Smart."

"I have my moments." Preston held me tighter. "This was done to you. That Loup did something to you. We'll fix it."

I shook my head. "Guys, listen to me. He is enormously powerful. I..." The need to run charged through me, and I growled. Anton approached fast. Like Preston, he stroked his finger over his mark. It did help. I had to finish what I was saying. "He killed all the Omegas like this. Made them sick. Crazy. They faded and died. The only person who could fix this would be me. And I can't do it. I have no power right now."

Jarret took me from Preston. I struggled but got nowhere with him either. My mind kept moving back and forth. Fight to stay, passive to aggressive. I couldn't keep track. I loved Jarret's arms around me, and yet the only thing I wanted to do was run away.

His pulse visibly pounded in his neck. It would be so easy to shift my teeth into fangs and tear apart his throat. I growled both at the thought and at the need to do so.

"Jarret." I struggled. "I might hurt you."

"Ssshh." He stroked the back of my hair. "No, you won't. You're stronger than this."

I'm glad he had so much faith in me, because I had none in myself. I closed my eyes, pressing my forehead to his shoulder. "I want to tear out your throat."

"That's okay, baby." Preston laughed. "We all want to do that on a regular basis."

I wasn't in the mood to laugh. I groaned instead.

Anton's mechanical voice spoke through the tablet. "I can find him. I guarantee it's in the books. When I wrote them, some things felt like... felt like I was compelled to write them, not because they belonged in the book, but because I had to. Like I had to tell someone what I knew. It was bizarre, and I took it as part of the writing process. Just a weird writing thing. But now I know... I have, stored in my head, things I don't even know I know. In here there has got to be his location."

The last thing I wanted was for them to go find him. "I don't think you have an appreciation for how powerful he is."

"Oh, we do." Rainer growled. "We have a perfect fucking understanding. But put this in your head somewhere and don't lose it: we will not lose our mate. You are ours. He will not take you from us. I don't care how many people I have to eliminate."

The sounds of cars outside caught their attention. I

didn't care. Let the cars come. Maybe I could escape in them and disappear into the swamp where no one would find me. Then I could be. I could have the anger. I could be... as I was meant to be.

"Humans," Preston said, staring out the window. He breathed in. "Those are cop cars."

Now that had my attention. "Why are the police here?"

"Not sure." Rainer nodded toward Jarret. "I assure you the bodies are buried. No one is going to find them."

Ross. It was hard for me to not think he'd had something to do with this.

A knock sounded on the door. It was my brother. "Rainer, the police are here to see you. They want to question you about something. They have a warrant to come in if you don't come out."

Could they do that? I sagged against Jarret, coherence threatening to flee.

"Tell them I'm coming out." His shoulders stiffened. "I won't have them coming in here and causing trouble for everyone. Preston?"

Next to me, he nodded. "On it. Don't let them hold you. Call one of Kevin's people. They'll help, even though he's gone. We need you, and this could be Ross."

"Oh," his smile held no mirth, "I'm sure that it is. Anton, keep working on location. Jarret, do not let her hurt herself. Preston, those people downstairs are your responsibility. Do something useful with them."

I found my voice. "Rainer, maybe... maybe we've lost. Maybe it just comes down to that. We've lost."

He stared at me for a long moment. "MacKenzie Harper, I love you. You are my mate. And right now, someone is taking you from me, the same person who took us from you. In that time, you survived hell to rescue us.

Expect the same treatment. We'll burn the world down for you."

With a turn of his head, he left the room, heading downstairs toward the waiting police. I closed my eyes. Ross was older than I'd known it possible to be. He was a Loup Garou, and he'd survived the madness to come out stronger than any wolf before him. No Omega had ever survived him. Even with Jarret holding me like I mattered most to him in the universe, I doubted. I had madness in my mind now. It wanted me to leave. To run. To kill those who would keep me safe.

You can't win.

I growled. They had to let me go. I didn't belong here.

Rainer

I didn't fight them. The truth was, that as I kept my eyes lowered and didn't tear out the throats of every person currently keeping me from MacKenzie, I wasn't being submissive. It might look that way to them. Or not. They were humans. They didn't pay close enough attention to things like that. Always baring their necks to whatever predator was in the room.

I chose to leave them alone. They had no idea how powerful that made me over them. I never would understand them. Not even when I pretended to be them. How did they function without listening to all of their senses? I'd barely been able to get through a day. Then MacKenzie came and... It was hard to think of her back in the house without me. What was happening?

I loved that woman. I would not lose her. If she had to

heal herself, then we'd figure out a way for her to do it. End of story. I'd keep her locked up in the house until she was better. Women didn't become Loups. I'd never considered what happened to them. They clearly had the same feelings but... they went silent like that woman my mate saved. I'd thought it horrifying at the time, which just went to show, once again, that I had to be careful when I got judgy about things. I inevitably ended up on the other side of whatever situation I was in.

A human slid onto a seat across the table from me. I hadn't missed dealing with the human authorities. My now-dead biological father had once told me to keep my head down and out of trouble, so I never need face this again. I had.

"Mr. Lejeune." He stared at a file in front of him.

I almost corrected him. I was Harper now. But then I remembered that humans didn't understand anything about us, even so much as our existing, and I kept quiet. Okay. I'd be Lejeune today. That had been my mother's last name. That's how these things worked.

She and my fathers had taken that name and made it famous. First with their parties in the swamp, and the way they'd made everyone feel comfortable. Later, living through what had happened to Anton and a death had made them notorious. A Loup named Ross had taken two fathers from me, as well as my brother's voice. He wasn't taking my mate.

The human in front of me ran a hand through what was left of his hair. Balding. A human trait.

"I... I'm not sure why you're here."

Was that so? I still didn't say anything. I had the right to remain silent. They had the right to hope I didn't change my mind about the tearing-out-their-throats thing.

"You served your time. No trouble since. I'm confused."

I leaned forward, and he leaned back. I doubted he realized he'd just submitted to me. Such confused creatures. "You came to my brother's home with quite a display of power."

"You're a chef, right?"

"Used to be." These days I only cooked if MacKenzie needed to eat. All roads led to her. "Who did you get your orders from?"

He scratched his chin. "Mr. Lejeune, I'm very confused. I don't really..."

Ah, I understood. The Loup had controlled the humans. He'd done it before when they killed Kevin. Amazing abilities. He hadn't been able to take my mate without effort. I wondered what that cost him. And also, why he had done this now?

Well, he wanted me away from the house.

"Then I suggest you let me go." That was, unless they were going to trump up charges and keep me here for nothing. I'd gone to jail for nothing, so that Brennan could control my family. It might happen again. Only this time, I would survive it better because she needed me to. I would not break inside. Somehow, I would be the wolf my mate required, the kind of man she made me feel I could be.

"Yes, I guess we're going to let you go."

This had been a time suck. A way to keep me away from home. Ross must be coming. Or sending someone and didn't want me there.

I'd get home, but it would be too late. I knew that already. Truth was, I wasn't worried. My pack would take care of my mate. Preston, Jarret, and Anton would see to her safety.

And when I got home... I'd see to revenge.

AFTERWORD

Thank you so much for reading Pursued (The Swamp #2). Book 3, Caught, is coming soon. Please stay tuned for news on that. In the meantime, please turn the page to read about me and about my other books. Also, please join me in my reader room here: https://www.facebook.com/groups/rebeccasrandomness

ABOUT THE AUTHOR

As a teenager, I would hide in my room to read my favorite romance novels when I was supposed to be doing my homework.

I am the mother of three adorable boys and I am fortunate to be married to my best friend. I live in Austin Texas where I am determined to eat all the barbecue in town.

I am in love with science fiction, fantasy, and the paranormal and try to use all of these elements in my writing. I've been told I'm a little bloodthirsty so I hope that when you read my work you'll enjoy the action packed ride that always ends in romance. I love to write series because I love to see characters develop over time and it always makes me happy to see my favorite characters make guest appearances in other books.

In my world anything is possible, anything can happen, and you should suspect that it will.

I'd love to hear from you! Please visit my website at www.rebeccaroyce.com to sign up for my newsletter and learn about my books!

Here's where you can find me online:

Rebecca's Randomness Reading Group https://www.facebook.com/groups/RebeccasRandomness/

https://www.rebeccaroyce.com

https://www.facebook.com/authorrebeccaroyce/

www.twitter.com/rebeccaroyce

Instagram: rebeccaroyce79
MeWe: RebeccaRoyce
Cheers!!
Rebecca

OTHER BOOKS BY REBECCA ROYCE...

Dragon Wars (completed series)

Forever

Eternal

Always

Evermore

Endless

Wards and Wands (completed series)

Hexed and Vexed

Curse Reversed

Meow, Baby (novella, co-written with Ripley Proserpina)

Tragic Magic

Safe Haven

Everywhere and Nowhere

Dimension X (coming soon)

More coming soon....

Soul Bound

Prisoner of the Dragons

More coming soon....

Shadow Promised

Strange Days

Weird Nights

Bizarre Years

More coming soon...

The Warrior (completed series)

Initiation

Driven

Subversive

Redemption

Justice

Warrior World (spin off of The Warrior, completed series)

Deacon

Micah

Jason

The Westervelt Wolves (completed series)

Her Wolf

Summer's Wolf

Wolf Reborn

Wolf's Valentine

Wolf's Magic

Alpha Wolf

Angel's Wolf

Darkest Wolf

Lone Wolf

Fallen Alpha

Alpha Rising

Alpha's Strength

Alpha's Sacrifice

Alpha's Truth

Alpha Enticing

Hidden Alpha (coming soon)

The Capes (completed series)

Seductive Powers

Adrenaline Rush

Last Ascension

Illicit Minds

Illicit Senses

Illicit Connections

Illicit Alliance (coming soon)

The Outsiders

Love Beyond Time

Love Beyond Sanity

Love Beyond Loyalty

Love Beyond Sight

Love Beyond Expectations

Love Beyond Oceans

Love Beyond Flames

Love Beyond Lies

Love Beyond Death (coming soon)

Cascade (completed series)

Haunted Redemption

Phoenix Everlasting

Fragility Unearthed

Persuasion Enraptured

Reverse Harem Story (completed series)

Unconventional

Unexpected

Undeniable

Kiss Her Goodbye (completed series)

Hard Truths

Dark Truths

Deadly Truths

Shifter World

Planet Bear

Planet Wolf (coming soon)

The Swamp

Hidden

Pursued

Caught (coming soon)

Stand Alone Titles

Under The Lights

No Quitting Allowed

Mr. Wrong

Bite Marks

Bitten Surrender

The Vampire and The Virgin

Demon Within

Crimson Lust

Call Me Crazy

The Storm (writing with Ripley Proserpina) **completed series.**

Lightning Strikes

Thunder Rolling

The Deluge

Heart of the Nebula (writing with Heather Long)

Queenmaker

Deal Breaker

Throne Taker (coming soon)

Stupid Boys (writing with C.R. Jane)

Stupid Boys

Dumb Girl (coming soon)

Through the Gates (writing with Skye MacKinnon)

Purgatory City

Infernal Land (coming soon)

The Coveted (writing with Ripley Proserpina)

Eyes in the Darkness

Voices in the Darkness (coming soon)